REACHING THE SUMMIT

Written By Dana Burkey
Edited By Brittany Morgan Williams

This book is first and foremost dedicated to my amazing and talented editor Brittany Morgan Williams.

Additional thanks Jan, Karen, Tabitha, and The Zerbes family for your constant encouragement throughout this project!

A HUGE thank you to the Etsy shops MySIXChicks for creating the equally as amazing bows for the back and CraftyOhBows for creating the perfect bows for the book cover. More information for each of these shops can be found at the back of the book.

Finally, thanks to all of my friends and readers on YouTube, Instagram, Goodreads, and FierceBoards for your never ending support and enthusiasm!

CHAPTER 1

"Continuing the awards for junior level 3," a man onstage said into a microphone. He opened a piece of paper covered in scores and results. "In third place we have-"

As expected he paused to add suspense. It gave me a minute to look around at the girls sitting in a circle around me. They were all dressed the same as I was in a red, black, and white TNT Force uniform. Like me, they all had on thick layers of makeup, and piles of curled hair surrounding their sparkly cheer bow. Like me they had been at the competition all weekend, competing first on

Saturday morning and then again Sunday afternoon. And, like me, they knew that once again we weren't going to finish in first place.

"From Wichita Falls, Texas," the announcer finally continued, "TNT Force Blast."

I stood up and cheered with the girls around me, trying to be proud of what we had done. We came in third. It was still one of the 'top' spots. But, with only four teams in our division to begin with, the win wasn't as sweet as it could have been. But, as Nicole and the other coaches at TNT had taught us to, we graciously accepted our medals and banners, taking a team photo before leaving the stage as the other teams were called for higher awards. Girls around me stopped to watch and see who would take home first, but all I was focused on was finding my dad.

"Third place. Not bad," my dad grinned before pulling me in for a hug. "Chin up Max. You did good out there, all things considered, sweetie."

"Yeah," I replied, knowing no one else could hear his little pep talk. "I just wish everyone else did too."

"None of that," he said evenly, obviously not happy with my mood. "The season's still not over."

I nodded while stepping back, showing him my best attempt at a smile. It was frustrating, not winning for the third competition in a row and all. But, he was right. We were trying our best to work through the changes in the routine. For Lexi and myself it was proving easy, but for some of the other girls the changes made the routine inconsistent and led to falls during competitions.

"Nitro performs in 40 minutes, so you have a little time until you need to be at the stage," Nicole, the coach of Blast and one of the gym owners explained to me and everyone around me. The team had all finally made its way to the door of the awards room after the rest of our division was announced. "And great job today ladies. We have some things to polish this week, but next weekend is a new chance to show the improvement we've made since NCA."

As Nicole began talking to some of the girls closest to her, I smiled as my best friends Lexi and Halley walked my way. They both were carrying their wallets, hinting it was time for us to go get bows. I handed my dad my bright red cheer bag then joined them as we headed out of the awards room. We walked to the back of the main auditorium where there were three tables selling bows. I didn't really care about the bows as much as I knew Halley or Lexi did, but I had adopted their tradition weeks prior. If we won the competition, then we would sit with our team and celebrate, taking selfies with our medals and anything else we won like championship sweaters, trophies, or buttons. But, if we lost, we would buy a cheer bow to raise our spirits. And thanks to the inconsistencies in our performances, my bow collection was growing more and more every weekend.

"How about this one?" Lexi asked, holding up a blue sequined bow to the red TNT Force bow that was in place around her curled white-blond hair. The color matched her eyes and really made them pop despite the red glitter she had piled on her eyelids. This might have also been because Lexi was still skinny and short enough, much like myself, that everything looked 'cute' on her. She could pull off even the most girly and glittery looks and styles with ease.

"Cute, but what about this one?" Halley reached up to hold a different bow to Lexi's hair, this one a glittery white bow with green words that read 'Cheer Queen' in glittery letters. The bow came complete with a little glittery crown in the center. If Lexi didn't want it, I knew Halley would likely snag it for herself.

Her hair was a shade darker than Lexi's, but the same colored bows still looked great on her, and just about every color matched her dark brown eyes and tan skin.

While they went back and forth making suggestions, I began looking for my own bow. Looking by myself was always best since I knew I wouldn't be choosing something with so much glitter. I had team bows that were covered in glitter and rhinestones, but when I was buying bows on my own, I always went for a solid color without too much decoration or writing. It made Lexi pout, but I always tried to explain that I couldn't pull off certain colors with my light brown hair. Hot pinks and bright greens didn't look as good on me as they did on both of my friends who were similar shades of bright blonde.

The real reason, however, was that I was still a tomboy all the way. Sure, I was on a cheer team and had to get all dolled up for competitions, but when I wasn't at the gym I would never be seen in clothes with rhinestones or sparkles. A few people told me they were sure I would act more girly eventually due to the cheerleading influence, but in the months since I joined the gym I was still just as big of a tomboy as I was before I started to cheer. When I wasn't at cheer I never wore makeup, spent any time doing my hair, or put any thought into what I was wearing. That was how I liked it though, and it helped me always feel comfortable.

"Look!" Lexi announced, grabbing a neon pink bow with glittery black letters. "We can get a matching set."

Before I could interrupt and explain that I didn't want a glittery bow, I realized what the bows said. It was a set of three bows, spelling out 'Best 'Friends' 'Forever.' The letters were in black and had a silver sparkly heart behind the words, on either a pink, green, or blue neon ribbon. Despite the glitter, when I saw the bows, I couldn't help but agree with Lexi. We bought the bows right away, although we knew we couldn't wear them until after we left the competition arena for good. It was a TNT rule that we all stayed in our uniforms, makeup, and even cheer hair until the whole day was over. The bows would likely be worn if we had a slumber party or all went together to the indoor trampoline park where I had met the girls only a few months ago.

"Let's go get something to eat before Nitro performs," Halley suggested, done with shopping once we had all paid for our bows.

"Do you think they're going to win today?" Lexi asked, linking arms with me and

Halley as we walked back towards where we knew the rest of our gym was sitting.

"They have a good shot," I commented. "Their raw score has everyone else beat. So, as long as they hit their double around to tick tock then they should be fine."

"You know their routine a little too well sometimes," Lexi laughed, nudging me with her arm. "I mean, I know you practice with them sometimes on your flying, but I think if you watched Connor perform much more you could fill his spot in the routine."

"I'm not watching them perform to see Connor," I replied.

"No, but he wants you to be there to watch him," Halley said before I could say anything more.

"I guess," I shrugged. "He said it would be cool to be on the same squad one day."

"And she is just as clueless as ever," Lexi said to Halley, both of them laughing at my confusion.

Thankfully I was saved from more of their laughter or comments as I made it to my dad. He was holding out a bag of trail mix, knowing I was likely going to be looking for a snack. Like always he was wearing his bright red shirt that read "CHEER DAD" on the front and "GO MAX" on the back, all in glittery silver letters. He got odd looks from people around town when he wore it from time to time, but around everyone at the gym it was expected and loved. The shirt made it easy for everyone to find him, and when they did, he was always ready to hand out treats for those in need.

"Do you still have Twizzlers?" Halley asked, plopping down into a chair while drinking from her red TNT water bottle.

"You're in luck," my dad grinned before handing her a bag containing just a few final red candies. "The Skittles, Reese's Pieces, and Oreos are all gone. It's just the Twizzlers, the trail mix, and the beef jerky left."

"We better save the jerky for Connor," I commented, which of course caused Halley and Lexi to make faces at one another and giggle once again. I did my best to ignore them. "How long until they perform?"

"You have about 10 minutes," he replied, after a glance at the schedule he was holding. "And then Bomb Squad performs just before final awards right at 5."

I nodded then sat down to snack on the trail mix. Pulling my phone out of my backpack, I saw I had three missed snapchats from Peter. I knew there would be more if I didn't reply soon, but I also didn't feel like starting a conversation with him only to run off and watch Nitro perform. Peter was usually at my competitions to cheer me on, but since we were in Dallas for the two-day event, he and his brother Kyle stayed home. Although they were only my neighbors, they were also basically my brothers, so I knew I would have to update Peter before too long. I snapped one photo to upload to my story announcing we got third, hoping that it would keep Peter satisfied for at least a little while. Then, I found myself distracted on Instagram until Lexi spoke.

"We should go," she announced to Halley and me, drawing my attention away from my phone. Since Lexi's brother Matthew was also on Nitro, getting a good spot to watch the routine was always important for her and her parents.

Tucking my phone back into my bag I stood up and followed the sea of red, black, and silver uniforms that was heading to the front of the room to stand right in front of the stage where Nitro would be performing in just a few seconds. As I stood between Halley, Lexi, and the other girls on Blast I also spied athletes from the other teams at TNT. We were easy to spot since everyone in our gym wears the same uniform, the only difference being the stripes of color that matched our team bows. Blast was red, Bomb Squad was pink, and Detonators were lime green, just to name a few. As Nitro, the teal team, was announced and took to the stage, I ignored the people around me and focused on Connor and the other athletes preparing to perform. If my team couldn't take home first, I at least wanted one of the teams from my gym to walk away winners. Since I couldn't help them accomplish that directly, I instead put everything into cheering as loud as possible for the entire 2-and-a-half-minute routine. I knew it might make me lose my voice, but after losing the competition, I didn't care too much at this point.

CHAPTER 2

"Run it again ladies," Nicole yelled out the following night at Blast team practice. "We're going to do it until we hit everything."

I let out a long breath and got back to my place for the start of the routine. After a long time stretching and doing some conditioning, we ran a few parts of the extremely familiar cheerleading routine before beginning full outs. Full outs, as I learned when I first joined the gym, meant we ran the whole routine from top to bottom as if we were performing for an audience. Most practices we would do only 1 or 2 full outs towards the end of our scheduled time then call it a night. But, after yet another less than great performance at the competition in Dallas, we were going until everything hit, which is just cheerleading lingo for doing it all perfect. It sounded like an okay task when Nicole presented it to us, but after 3 full outs, everyone was starting to lose confidence. I found myself doubting we could ever perfect every skill even once.

"Smiles on everyone," Halley said to me with an exaggerated facial expression.

"I doubt we're going to have to run it again if I don't smile," I said evenly. "We'll have to run it again when Lara can't stay in the air."

"Maybe she'll hit this time," Halley tried again, her smile fading a little.

Before we could discuss the issue any further, the routine started. I performed my opening back tuck and dance moves before moving to stand with my stunt group for my first flying skill. The girls in my stunt group were all a bit taller than me, which helped a lot in the moves we performed on the mat. Halley, along with Anna, Skylar, and Olivia lifted me into the air on one leg so I could hold my left foot next to my head in a basic move known as a heel stretch. Knowing I didn't want to be responsible for not running a perfect routine, I faked a smile as the girls brought me back to the ground, just in time for me to do a round off and back tuck before walking towards them and stepping right back into their arms for my next flying move called a liberty. It was a move where I stood on one leg, with my other leg bent so my foot was next to the knee of my straight leg. It was an easy skill, but it was the moves that followed it that had me worried for the other girls in the air. Out of the corner of my eye, I watched the other four fliers all holding the same pose as me. Then, as we all held our legs up near the back of our heads with both arms in a move called a scorpion, the stunt team below us turned us so we were facing stage right instead of looking at the crowd, I saw not one but two of the fliers fall into the arms of their stunt groups below them. It looked like we would be running the routine yet again. And possibly again after that as well.

"Should we stop and get ice cream?" my dad asked an hour later as we were driving home from practice. After sitting and watching from the parent's lounge through the 5 full outs that still never managed to hit, he knew I needed a pick me up.

"Did you really have to ask?"

"Double hot fudge sundae with sprinkles?" he smiled, turning his truck automatically towards our favorite ice cream shop in town.

"I might need triple hot fudge after that," I sighed, pulling my ombre red cheer bow out of my hair. I was too hot to pull on anything over my glittery TNT Force tank top or short red practice shorts, so losing the bow was going to have to be good enough for now. When the weather was a little cooler I would slip on basketball shorts over my practice uniform, but the Texas heat was too intense to worry about it just then. Even after three years I was struggling to adjust to the hot southern weather after moving from the Oregon coast.

"You did really great tonight Max," he reminded me.

"I know," I replied. "I hit 4 out of the 5 times we ran it full out. But if no one else can get it right then it doesn't matter."

"Lexi got everything all 5 times," he noted as he parked his car in the familiar parking lot.

"Yeah, but that's only two of us really pulling our weight," I spoke while climbing out of the truck, eager for the ice cream to boost my spirits. "I don't think Jackie ever hit, and Brit bobbles so many times it might actually be a smaller deduction if she just dropped her stunt."

My dad listened to my complaints as we walked up to the outside window to order. We waited in silence for the ice cream, which was thankfully only a minute or two. Then, as we took a seat at one of the picnic tables near the building, my dad began what I assumed was a long and thought out speech.

"If you're only cheering to win, then I think you're in the wrong sport," he began, pausing to eat a large spoonful of his sundae. "Now I know some of the girls aren't doing as well as you and Lexi, but I think some of that has to do with your extra classes. All the coaches have talked to me about how good your skills are, and how you're going to move up a level next year, and that's great. But not all of the girls on your team are going to be moving up next year, and that's okay too. Some of them are still learning and trying their hardest. So while you're on the team you need to understand that you can be encouraging them and cheering people on. If you want to be on a different squad next year, then you can do that. But until then it's a team sport and you win and lose as a team. You've been on basketball teams that have lost almost every game and you made it through the season. I know you can do it this time too."

"But when I was on a basketball team that was bad I could still do my best and score some points and feel like I made a difference," I challenged him, annoyed that he had basically just called out my bad attitude.

"And you can do that while you're cheering as well," he replied immediately. "You and Lexi are staying in the air and doing all the moves, so that's helping on the score sheet. And you and Corral tumbling is better than any team in your division I've seen all year."

I was a little shocked to hear my dad explain various elements of our routine so easily. Just five months ago neither of us knew the difference between a heel stretch and a full. But over the past few months as I learned skills in my team practices and extra classes, my dad was chatting with other parents and understanding the various elements of all star cheerleading as well. Even still, as weird as it was for me to know all the ins and outs of the cheer world, it was even weirder to hear him talking about it so easily.

"What if we don't win any more this season?" I finally asked. "What if we make fools of ourselves?"

"Not possible," he assured me. "You guys started the season strong and people will remember that. The routine was easier then, but it got you a wild card bid to Summit and that's what matters. Some teams work all season and don't get to go to Summit at all."

"But we might go to Summit and be the worst team there," I tried again.

"Then out of all the top teams you're not the best," he shrugged. "You ladies are still good and you prove that every time you hit the mat. The changes Nicole made to the routine are hard for your level, and getting them to hit will take time. But you have three weeks after this weekend to clean it all up. It's plenty of time to work out all the stumbling blocks."

"I guess," I said with a sigh.

"I never thought I would see this day," my dad laughed. When I gave him a confused look he continued. "Here's my little Max, stressing about whether or not she will be the best cheerleader in the land."

"Funny, Dad," I said with a smile despite trying to keep it in. "I'm just an athlete trying to do my best."

"And you'll do your best," he said earnestly. "But for right now you need to do your best while still staying positive even if some of the girls around you are still learning and trying. One of these days you might be on a team where you're the low man on the totem pole and it won't feel very nice if someone is less than encouraging just because they are better than you at a tick tick or a heel pull."

"Tick tock and heel stretch," I corrected him, knowing he had messed up on purpose. "And who said I'm even going to do cheer after this year?"

"You might not," he said around a bite of ice cream. "But if you decide to leave that gym I know you'll miss it too much to stay gone for long."

I didn't say it, but I knew he was kind of right. Lexi and Halley were my best friends other than Peter and Kyle. After helping me through fitting in at the gym when I was new and felt like I would never have things in common with the other kids there, I knew they were going to be friends of mine forever, just like our new cheer bows said. But, at the same time, the idea of failing at a big competition like Summit was not exactly appealing. It was the biggest competition a level 3 team like Blast could make it to, so even getting invited was a big deal. All of that wouldn't matter much, however, if we got there and couldn't keep stunts in the air enough to even make it to day two, let alone the final round. I tried to push the stress of that thought to the back of my mind and instead focus all my energy on the quickly melting sundae in front of me.

CHAPTER 3

I was thankful for a few days off of Blast practice but was still back in the gym Tuesday evening for my extra skills class. The class was usually held on Fridays, but when we had competitions on the weekend, the class was moved around so we didn't get overworked or even hurt the day before competing. I hadn't always been a part of the class, but once the school year started, I was asked to join Greg and a group of athletes for the extra practice after I had stopped attending my initial tumbling class. It gave me a chance to try harder tumbling, work on flying, and also help some of the guys at the gym work on lifting me up and holding me in the air. Walking into the large open space, I tossed my bag into a cubby by the first of four blue mats that ran the length of the room. There was a wall of mirrors that ran the length of the far wall, although I knew we wouldn't use them much during our class. Facial expressions and spacing were the last things on our mind during our skills class.

I gave my dad a quick wave as he walked into the parent viewing area and started instantly talking to someone he knew. There was only a dozen or so adults in the room at the moment, although more would be arriving for team practices soon. Parents were allowed in the gym only if they were inside the viewing room, almost like a little parent zoo for us athletes to look at from time to time. When I asked TJ, one of the gym owners, about it once, he told me, "Cheer moms can be mean and nasty when they get right down to it." I didn't really know what that meant, but after a whole season of competitions where I would watch the way some moms talked to their children as well as the coaches, I was thankful for the viewing room. I was also extra thankful for my dad. Sure, it was a bummer my mom wasn't around to see me following in her footsteps with cheerleading, but having my dad cheer me on without ever stressing me out was a real big plus!

Walking closer to Greg, I sat down and started stretching. Greg was a good bit older than me, having already aged out of the TNT gym once he graduated high school. Not to mention he also finished four years cheering in college before he began coaching at the gym. But, even being 'old' compared to me and a lot of the athletes at TNT, Greg was still in great shape. He was around 6 feet tall and well-built from his years of holding fliers in the air. He had short black hair and a layer of black stubble on his face and grayish-blue eyes that when combined with his height and muscles could be a little intimidating, to say the least. Thankfully, after working alongside him for so long on my tumbling, he was like a big brother I was glad to be around. Even when we had to work hard on something, he made it fun for everyone, all while pushing us to really reach our potential.

"So, what are we working on tonight?" I asked him as I started doing some of the harder stretches that would get me ready for the skills I was about to perform.

"I want you to work on getting more height on that kick full," Greg said with a determined look on his face. "You're not quite high enough off the ground without the air mat to get the second rotation, but I think you're not too far from it."

"What about her standing double full?" someone said, walking over to join us. "When are we going to see her land that?"

"Soon enough," I assured Connor once he sat down in my field of vision. I was bent pretty far backward while in a split so I could stretch my back and arms, so until he took a seat I wasn't quite sure who had been talking.

"I think you're going to get it before I do," he said with a smile.

"Fingers crossed," I nodded, knowing our back and forth banter was all in fun.

Connor was, after all, my best guy friend in the gym. He was the first person I got to know other than Halley and Lexi, and was just as close to me as Peter and Kyle, even though I hadn't known him nearly as long. Connor was only two years older than me, but he was a lot taller and stronger than most 15-year old's I knew. This was likely because, much like Greg, he spent a lot of time lifting fliers into the air for stunts while at the gym. Also, like Greg, he had dark brown hair, although Connor's tended to curl as it got longer. When I first met him his hair was a little longer so the curl was easy to see, but once competition season started he cut his hair shorter with just a little bit of a spiked up section in the front, which only helped to draw attention to his dark green eyes. The main thing people noticed when they looked at Connor, however, were his dimples. He always seemed to be smiling, and when he did, his dimples were all you could focus on. Before I met him I had always thought my dimples were noticeable, but standing next to Connor, mine were all but nonexistent.

"Okay, time to get started," Greg announced after Matthew, Reid, and Gwen all arrived. "Let's start with some basic stunts."

The one thing that was a little exhausting about my skills class was that I was the only flier, surrounded by athletes much taller and stronger than I was. Sure, we were all there to work on our tumbling with Greg as well, since he was the gym's head tumbling coach, but everyone besides me was there to work on basing. That meant that I was constantly up in the air working on new skills or holding poses I had already mastered in my time on Blast. I would hold an arabesque or a scorpion, or even try to hold one leg as flat as possible to my back in a position known as a needle, which was a newer move for me. As soon as I held the move for another count or so, I would be brought down to the mat. Then, I would be picked up once again to try the move with a new person or group of people lifting me. It helped them that I was the smallest 13-year-old at the gym by at least 6 inches and easily 15 pounds. I used to complain that I was still well under 5 feet tall, but my time at cheerleading was helping me to embrace it more and more. After all, thanks to my small frame, the other athletes in my stunt class could lift and toss me effortlessly, all while I got to work on my flying skills in the air. The practice allowed me to get used to smaller stunt groups and even one-on-one partner stunting, all of which developed my balance for when I was flying with my stunt group on Blast.

"Explain to me again why you're not on a senior team yet," Gwen joked after working with Reid to toss me up for a kick double down. The move was a harder version of one we did on my junior level 3 team, only with an added rotation thrown in to make the move a harder stunt. When Gwen and Reid, who were both on a senior level 5 team, tossed me into the air I kicked one leg up by my head while keeping the other straight. Then, on the way down, I wiped my body around twice before I landed safely in their arms.

"I've only been cheering for a few months," I reminded her.

In response, Gwen rolled her eyes and gave her long brown hair a dramatic flip. We both laughed since Gwen and I learned early on while practicing together that we were both tomboys. It was hard to believe it looking at Gwen in her hot pink shorts, TNT tank top with glittery pink letters, and matching hot pink cheer bow. But, much like me, she only looked the part thanks to the gym wardrobe rules. Gwen was on her school's soccer team and was one of the best goalies in the state. And sure, playing soccer didn't make you a tomboy, but it was just one of the many things I learned about her that made me realize we were so much alike. Although she was 4 years older than me, we had gotten to become good friends through our time together in the weekly skills class.

"Want to run it again?" Reid asked. He ran a hand through his sweat-drenched hair, messing up the fauxhawk he had styled before practice. It was clear he was trying to keep us on track as Gwen and I continued to laugh, but that was easier said than done.

"Water break," Gwen said with a shake of her head once she and I were done laughing.

While Reid and Gwen walked to grab their water bottles, I headed over to the air mat to work on my tumbling. It reminded me of an air mattress I used while camping, only built a little differently to give you extra bounce when working on a new trick. The spring loaded mats we performed on weren't bad, but during my skills class, I loved getting to use the air mat. It was like a perfect mix between the trampoline running track and actually being on a hard floor.

I wasn't that tired after the flying we'd done in skills class, so I was happy to try some tumbling to really get in a good workout. Sure, I had to really 'lock my core' as Greg and Tonya always told me, but thanks to all the conditioning and practices at the gym it was pretty easy. I knew if Tonya, one of the gym owners and coaches, was at our skills practice she would make me work on stretches until Gwen and Reid were ready to do more flying again. But as much as I loved to be up in the air flying, I loved tumbling even more. So, without her there to keep me focused on just flying, I happily stepped onto the air mat to try out a few things I had been working on.

Giving myself a running start, I did a round off, then immediately launched myself into a back handspring and then a whip. The whip was more or less just a back tuck without the tuck, so as I flipped around and landed, I was able to push off a little harder for the final movement in the tumbling pass. Spinning in the air, I twisted my body around twice as fast I could, while also completing a backflip motion. The result of the two moves combined was a double full, which I almost landed. My toes hit the ground but the momentum of the move had me falling down onto my knees before I could firmly plant my heels on the ground. I let out a frustrated sigh and stood up to try it again.

"That was good height," Greg said walking over to me. "Why don't you try throwing a second whip in there before the full for a little extra power?"

I nodded at Greg and tried again, this time doing two whips before trying the double full. I landed it easily that time, but then again, things were always a little easier when tried on the air mat. Moving to stand on the normal gym floor, I began trying the same series of moves on the blue spring-loaded mats that would be under me during competition. Knowing it would be a little harder to get high enough for the double full on the normal cheer floor, I tried a standard full a few times before trying the double. Each time I failed Greg would tell me how to move my body a little differently to get it right, or encourage me that I almost had it. When I applied his advice I could see the changes immediately. Thanks to my time in his skills class Greg had become like a big brother to me. He was closer in age to me than my coach, Nicole, or the other gym owners, but was still almost 30. Although, you wouldn't know that by how he acted in the gym. Especially since he could still do all the tumbling he taught in his class. It shocked me at first to see him do kick fulls and double backflips, but when I learned more about his all star and college cheer experience, it made a little more sense.

"Okay," I finally breathed after trying the tumbling pass a few more times. "I need water."

"Good thinking," Greg nodded. "Then let's go back to flying for a little. That should give you a break."

I agreed easily, then grabbed my water bottle for a quick drink. After over an hour of working on different skills, I was thirstier than I realized. I quickly downed most of my water but stopped before finishing it off. Drinking that much might be a bad idea before I got thrown into the air, so I closed my water bottle's cap then turned to get back on the mat.

"Let's try some partner stunts for a while," Greg said as I rejoined the group in the center of the mat. "Max just do a lib to start. Then, if that goes okay we can try a heel stretch tick tock and also a scorpion to arabesque."

"Got it," I smiled, the terms that were so confusing just a few months ago now simple and easy to follow. The idea of only one person holding me in the air was also something that would have been daunting not too long ago but was fast becoming no big deal. "Alright, who's first?" I said to Gwen, Reid, Matthew, and Connor, ready to get picked up once again.

CHAPTER 4

"So what do you think, seven full outs tonight before we hit?" Lexi asked me as we grabbed a drink. We had just finished the conditioning portion of our practice on Thursday evening. We spent a lot of time going over our standing jump sequence, but tried it using rubber bands around our feet to make it a little harder. In general, we had good height on our toe touches and hurdlers, but it was always good to work on the stretching that went with the moves as well.

"My bet's nine," I replied to Lexi's question, already preparing for a lot of stunt falls from the other girls.

"At least." Halley agreed. "I'm not really looking forward to Saturday too much right now."

Lexi and I nodded in agreement as Nicole called the team back on the mat. I sat with Halley and Lexi to my left, and Anna to my right. We were a sea of black, white, and red, all of us in our matching practice uniforms and red bows. With 30 of us in total, it took a moment for us to settle down. Once we did, we were shocked at what Nicole had to tell us.

"We're making some changes for this weekend," Nicole said, her voice as serious as the look on her face. She was not a very tall woman, but she was intense all the same. Nicole had fiery red hair that was a tangle of curls that only made her bright green eyes pop even more. She was thin and muscular, still showing the strength she developed during years of all star cheerleading. Although she was wearing her glittery TNT Force staff shirt and jeans, it might as well have been a power suit. She was all business as she looked over us girls for a few seconds before continuing. "If we can't hit the skills we have in the routine right now, then we need to take them out. So we're going to water down your elite flying, take out some of the tumbling, and then we will see if we need to change any of pyramid. It's going to be a little harder than the routine we started the season with, but not quite the level we were going for last weekend."

Around me, girls instantly began talking. I could hear girls chatting about how shocked they were since they were just getting used to the new changes. I also heard someone say how hard and long practice was going to be. But then, I heard a few people say they were excited since it meant they might finally stay in the air while flying or land all of their tumbling. As soon as I heard that my hand shot up in the air, desperate for answers.

"Yes, Max?" Nicole called on me, quieting the rest of the group.

"If we water down the routine then we won't have a chance to win at Summit," I said simply, having gone over our raw score compared to most other teams in our division at least a dozen times. I always loved looking at batting averages, team rankings, and stats for any sports teams I was a part of. So, with cheer, I would sit at home and watch YouTube videos and check score sheets to see how well a team did, and how much better they could have done if everything went as planned. I knew that by taking hard elements out of the Blast routine, there were at least two teams we would compete against at Summit that would have a higher raw score. Summit, an international competition in Florida, was the last competition of the season and winning first there had been the goal all year.

"Right now we need to focus on a clean routine," Nicole explained, a look of defeat on her face. "If we can't hit the basics then we will never have a chance to hit the harder skills we've been planning."

"But our raw score," I began again, only to be cut off.

"Everyone get in positions for your elite flying and then we'll go over the changes," Nicole said before turning to me. "Max, can I talk to you for a minute."

I gave Lexi and Halley a confused look, but they just shrugged and moved to stand in the places Nicole had directed. I noticed that Tonya was now on the mat as well, talking to the first of the stunt groups, and likely explaining the new motions to the flier. Since Tonya was the gym's main flying coach it made sense that Nicole brought her in to help us rework the routine. Pushing those thoughts aside, I followed Nicole off the mat, not sure what she was going to say.

"I understand you're frustrated, Max," she said finally. "And I feel the same way. But for some of these girls, it's hard to do moves that come easily to you. They just can't stay in the air. And I would rather them stay up and feel like they did their best at what they can do, then to fall and fail. If we hit a clean routine and still don't win at least we can say we did what we planned to accomplish. But if we push it super hard and lose, then it won't build up their confidence at all."

"So we're going to admit defeat, and just choose what form of defeat we accept?" I asked, trying to sum up all that I had just heard.

"No," Nicole began again. "We have girls on this team that will be on a level 3 team for another year or two. They can't push to places you can. They don't have skills that you have. We started the season out by hitting a routine, winning a bid to Summit, and everyone felt great. But then when we started to make it harder we learned we aren't quite ready for that. Maybe next year we can make the routine harder and push the team more. But for now, all we can do is work at our skill level and make it clean. I know it's not the easiest decision to make, but it's the best one for everyone on the team."

I noticed she said a lot of the same things my dad had said after the last Blast practice. In response, I simply nodded. But inside, I was screaming. No matter what sport I was playing or what game I was trying, I was competitive. Losing wasn't fun, even if it was at something as new to me as cheerleading. I knew this was likely because for me all of the flying and tumbling was super easy. The extra classes and time in the gym working with Gary and Tonya and my friends from higher level teams like Connor and Gwen helped even harder skills to be basically second nature. Finally, I walked back to where my stunt group was waiting. I tried to control my frustration though, and not let it show to the other girls.

"We're just doing a lib and then a heel stretch before the arabesque," Halley filled me in quickly

"We're taking out the tick tock in the lib?" I asked, certain she forgot to mention it.

"Yes," Halley nodded, looking rather dejected. "We're also taking out the scorpion and your tumbling into the basket."

"Tonya said even if Nicole changes things in the pyramid, your part should still be the same," Olivia quickly said, likely noticing the look on my face.

"Okay girls," Nicole called out after Tonya had spoken to everyone and stepped off the mat. "From the top of this section. 5-6-7-8."

I spent the rest of the evening trying my best to put on a fake smile and work on the routine with the changes. I was still doing all of the same tumbling I had been working on all season, but with changes in my flying, it was hard to have a good attitude. Instead of holding my leg up in the scorpion I was used to, I was simply standing on one leg in the lib, or liberty pose. It was just one of the many things I had to do instead of the harder moves I had worked so hard to learn. Nicole called out encouragements as we worked on learning the easier routine, then ran everything full out a few times. Everyone was having a much better time staying in the air, and we even hit the routine without mistakes on only the third try. It proved the changes were a good idea, but still did little to help me feel happy about all of them.

"Good job today Max," Tonya said to me as I was packing up my gym bag after practice was over.

"Thanks," I said to Tonya, although I'm certain my facial expression didn't match my words. I was too bummed about everything to fake it any longer. And, as if dealing with everything wasn't bad enough, I was, of course, stopped by a familiar face before I could make it to where my dad was waiting for me near the door.

"The routine looks really cute," Leanna said, flashing me an exaggerated smile. "For a second there I thought I was watching a level 2 team performing."

Ever since I first met Leanne at a private practice shortly after I joined the gym, I got the sense she didn't like me much. She was always quick to shoot glares at me, make rude comments, and especially roll her eyes. Unlike when Gwen rolled her eyes, Leanne was always annoyed and serious in her disdain for me. I had observed her rolling her eyes at other people and even making not so nice comments here and there, so I got the feeling it was just her personality. But, knowing that still did little to make me warm up to her.

Part of the reason could have been that everything about Leanne seemed a little forced and fake to me. Even when she was at the gym for practices she wore more makeup than some girls I saw at competition. Her blue eyes were always surrounded by thick layers of makeup and even fake eyelashes. It didn't help that her hair was so blond it was almost white, but not in the natural way that both Lexi and Matthews's hair looked. Her hair was bleached and teased and curled so big it was a lot to take in, especially against her skin. Like a lot of girls that I saw at cheer, Leanne spent time in the tanning bed to get ready for competition. But, unlike a lot of girls, Leanna didn't seem to know when to stop. Her tan was so dark and almost orange that, when added to her makeup and hair, it was impossible not to look at her. And not always in a good way. Sure, she was thin and muscular and only an inch or two taller than me, but her look was so over the top it seemed to get her attention for how out of place she looked even around other cheerleaders.

"We're just making a few changes for this weekend," I finally said to Leanna, knowing she was just looking for a way to make another comment. Like many times before, I got the feeling she was going out of her way to be petty.

"You did awesome," a voice said behind me. Turning, I was happy to see Connor walking up to me with a smile on his face. "You're going to hit for sure with the changes to the routine."

"Thanks, Connor," I smiled, glad for his vote of confidence, and also the distraction from Leanna's rude comments. "Are you ready for Saturday?"

"Saturday's going to be a breeze," Connor grinned, his face lighting up and drawing even more attention to his dimples, as always. "If we lose Saturday then it's no big deal. What I'm worried about is Worlds."

"You'll do great," I assured him quickly. "You've come in first or second all season. Everyone is saying you're a shoo-in for the finals."

"We better. We have to keep the gym's reputation good in case other teams fail," Leanne said with a fake smile before she walked towards the mat where the other members of Nitro were getting ready for practice. I knew she was making yet another comment about Blast and the fact we hadn't been doing great all season but chose to ignore it since at least she was walking away from me.

"I should get going," I said, knowing Connor's practice would be starting soon.

"See you Saturday," Connor said to me before I turned to head out of the gym. "Oh, and Max?"

"Yeah?" I asked, pausing to face him again.

"Even if you don't get to show it when you fly with the new routine, everyone is going to see how amazing you are when you tumble."

I nodded in response, a grin quickly growing on my face. It faded some when I noticed that Leanne was once again shooting me one of her death glares. Not wanting to join her in whatever bad mood she had found herself in once again, I simply gave Connor a goodbye wave and turned to walk to where my dad waiting for me.

CHAPTER 5

Before I started cheerleading I never once thought about my hair. I either pulled it in some kind of a ponytail or let it hang around my face without a thought. And it never bothered me. But then, I joined the TNT Force gym and realized that my hair was important. Not just my hair, but also my makeup and wardrobe. It was a lot to take in, and even more to learn. I had to wear my hair in a ponytail high enough to show off a bow, I needed to put on enough makeup for the judges to see it from across a dark and crowded room. All of that, as you might guess, is easier said than done. But it was all a part of the look. A look, that in the case of both my practice uniform and team uniform, was basically covered top to bottom with rhinestones and glitter.

"Dad, did you buy more hair spray?" I called from my bathroom. I was diligently trying to tease my hair bright and early on this Saturday morning.

"Under your sink," he called back. "We need to leave in half an hour."

Letting out a sigh, I opened the cupboard and pulled out a nice new can of mega hold hair spray. I coated my hair in it before attacking it again with my teasing comb. Doing my makeup in the car was easy enough, but my hair needed to be ready when I walked out the door. Lexi and Halley had spent a lot of time trying to teach me how to curl my hair with a wand, make a front 'poof,' and even put my bow in place without needing help. But every time I got ready before a competition, it still took a lot of effort. The only good thing was that after the hour car ride to the competition site, I would be able to get a little help touching up everything before I had to perform.

"Ready!" I called, racing out of the bathroom looking only half put together. I was wearing a short-sleeved black shirt with TNT

Force glittering on the front in silver and red letters, and a pair of black sweat pants. The look was quite a juxtaposition to my hair that was teased and styled into a mass of brown curls, all coated in a thick layer of hair spray.

"You're performing like that?" Kyle asked, glancing up in shock from where he sat on the couch.

"No," I said with a frown. "I have to do my makeup in the car."

Looking Kyle's way, I wasn't surprised to see he had both Thunder and Lightning sitting in his lap. The two kittens joined my family after my dad bribed me to give the cheer gym a try. At the time I assumed I would end up with two cats and no more cheerleading. Boy, was I wrong on that one. Kyle speaking to me had been loud enough to wake up both kittens, causing them to open their sleepy kitty eyes. After all, it was still only just after six in the morning. Thunder let out a yawn then tried to curl back up into a little gray ball and sleep. Lightning, however, began moving his small white and orange striped body around to get comfortable before trying to go back to sleep. I knew they were going to be moved and likely woken up again when it was time to leave, but they would get over it. They were still young enough that they slept often during the day; usually when they finally stopped running around the house and playing.

"I'll carry your bag," Peter offered as he walked into the room, picking up my glittery red gym bag that contained my uniform, makeup, and cheer shoes.

"Thanks," I breathed as I slipped on my matching glitter backpack and headed outside to start getting loaded into the car.

Checking my phone as I climbed into the back seat with Kyle a minute later, I saw that I had missed lot of texts from the girls in my stunt group. When we were traveling from home for competitions we always started the day with a chat to get us ready to perform. The chat was usually reminders about parts of the routine we struggled with in practice, songs we should listen to that would help us get pumped up, and of course lots of corresponding selfies on Snapchat. I was still working on getting good at selfies but snapped one with the note 'time for makeup in the car' so everyone knew why I wouldn't be texting for a little while longer.

"More selfies?" Peter asked, startling me. Looking up I saw he was smooshing his face between his seat and the side of the car so he was closer to me. I couldn't help but laugh at the sight of his face all scrunched up, framed by his curly black hair.

"Just one," I laughed. "I have to do my makeup now for real."

"Okay," he sighed, turning to face forward once again.

I began unpacking my makeup bag, lying the tools and products around me to be reached easily. Beside me, Kyle was in a world of his own playing games on his phone with his headphones and everything. Just when all of my makeup was laid out and I was ready to get started applying it, my phone went off. Assuming it was a photo from Halley or Anna, I opened Snapchat and was surprised to see a photo of Peter. It was an up close selfie, with mostly just his green eyes in the photo. They were crossed at such an extreme pose that I instantly had to stifle a laugh.

"Stop," I said trying not to smile. "I need to do my makeup."

Peter apologized, allowing me to get back to work. But, as I began to spread makeup over my face in thick strokes that would look bold and exciting even from across a room, I could hear my phone buzzing frequently with more messages from the front seat of the car. Trying my best to ignore them, I managed to get everything but my eyeliner and mascara done by the time we pulled into the quickly filling parking lot of the high school where we would be performing. I knew I would be able to coat on the mascara okay by myself, but even after trying over and over, I couldn't quite put on my eyeliner the way the other girls could. I always needed help to get both eyes to match, complete with winged out corners.

"You're here!" a voice called out as I was finally climbing out of the car.

Turning, I wasn't at all surprised to see Lexi skipping towards me. She was wearing the same outfit I was, only with a pair of short red shorts replacing my sweatpants. I gave her a hug then grabbed my bags, taking the one Peter had hauled into the car.

"Can you help me with my eyeliner?" I asked Lexi, knowing she would eagerly agree.

"Duh!" She laughed before linking her arm with mine and taking off towards the buildings' entrance.

"See you in there," I called behind myself, knowing my dad would find the other TNT cheer parents before too long.

"Are you going to answer that?" Lexi asked, noticing my buzzing phone before I did.

"Oh, it's just another Snapchat from Peter I bet," I sighed. "He was sending them the whole way here."

Opening my phone, I couldn't help but laugh at the image that popped up. Not only was Peter smiling in the photo, he was joined for the selfie by both Kyle and my dad. My dad stuck out in the photo, his skin much lighter than my neighbors, who got their dark tan skin from their Mexican heritage. As if that wasn't enough to make my dad stand out, his eyes looked more gray than green compared to the emerald colored eyes surrounding him. His hair was also looking extra gray in the photo. especially at the temples where his brown hair was less and less evident all the time. Kyle and Peter, on the other hand, had matching black hair that was curled up in tiny ringlets. If it wasn't for Peter's angular jaw and thinner face, Kyle could almost pass for his twin.

"Any messages from Connor?" Lexi asked, a strange look on her face after seeing the photo Peter had sent me.

"I don't think so," I said with a shrug before checking. "Oh. I have a few missed ones from him. And the group text."

Knowing I was about to see everyone, I slipped my phone back into my pocket and continued walking into the school. It wasn't worth the time to reply to messages when I had hair to fix and makeup to finish and a uniform to put on. And that was exactly what I did. Lexi, with her expert hair skills, touched up the curls that I hadn't gotten quite right. Halley helped me get the eyeliner applied to my lids in a perfect sweep that I still hadn't mastered. Then, she helped me get enough layers of mascara on to match everyone else on the team. It left me with just enough time to get my uniform on before we had to head to warm-ups.

Giving myself one last glance in the bathroom mirror after changing, I was happy to see I looked the part of an all star cheerleader once again. Our uniform skirts were black with thick white and red stripes along the bottom hem that was spotted with rhinestones. The top of the uniform was a long sleeved black shirt that had the same glittering white and red bands around the neck and down the sleeves, both dotted with sparkling rhinestones. On the chest of the uniform, much like all of the official clothing from the gym, the letters TNT Force were printed big and bold for everyone to see in glittery red and silver. The uniforms were simple compared to some of the other teams we went up against each weekend, but with the addition of the big hair, big bows, layers of makeup, and bold white cheer shoes, it was good enough for me.

"Selfie!" Halley announced the second I walked out of the bathroom. Much like buying bows when we lost, pre-warm up selfies were also a competition tradition. Like always, we snapped the photo and posted it on all of our social media accounts before following the rest of the girls on Blast as they walked towards the room where we were going to be stretching before warm-ups.

"Did you check your phone yet?" Lexi asked, peering over my shoulder as I posted the photo to my Instagram account.

"I'll do it now," I assured her, pulling up my messages. After skimming the latest in the group text, I pulled up the message from Connor and was happy to see his simple message.

"Win or lose, watered down or full force, you are one of the best cheerleaders I know, and I can't wait to see you kill it today!"

"How sweet!" Halley immediately said into my ear, clearly having read the text over my shoulder.

Ignoring her, and the looks Lexi was sending my way, I wrote a quick "thank you" to Connor before sliding my phone into my cheer bag. As expected, my dad was waiting to give me a hug and take my bags as we walked into our stretching area. I planted a quick kiss on his cheek then gave a high-five to both Peter and Kyle. Then, knowing I needed to get ready to take the stage, I followed after my friends and started preparing for the upcoming performance.

CHAPTER 6

"You did so great!" Connor called to me, rushing over to give me a hug. We were just exiting the stage after we had finished our performance. Hugging Connor was still strange to me since I wasn't a big hug person with anyone besides maybe my dad. But, my time at the gym was bringing it out of me more and more. "I think you're the only squad in your division to hit zero."

"Awesome," I agreed easily. Hitting zero meant we had no deductions. No bobbles, no stunt falls, and no missed tumbling passes. But I knew it was only because our raw score and difficulty were at a lower level to start with. It made doing so well bittersweet for sure.

I was hugged and high-fived by a few more people, some in the same teal uniform as Connor, others in pink, blue, purple, and orange. At the start of the season, it was weird for me to have people I didn't know congratulate me when I was done performing, but I had since learned that it was something all of the TNT Force athletes did for one another. Even if you didn't know a person by name, they were a part of your gym so you were expected to support them. And most people took that support seriously.

"You guys finally hit your routine," Leanne said to me, smiling in a way that looked both fake and somehow actually happy at the same time.

"Yup, and hopefully you guys hit later too," I said in reply, pretending her words were meant as a real compliment. "Oh, and before I forget," I said turning to Connor. "I loved the text you sent this morning. It was perfect."

As Connor thanked me, Leanne gave her perfectly curled hair a flip and stormed off. I wasn't exactly sure what had caused it, but wished I did so I could do it anytime she was bugging me. After all, her walking away always meant I didn't have to deal with her attitude anymore. But, before I could ask Connor if he knew what was up with her, the whole red team was ushered off to the viewing booth. It was little more than a TV monitor inside a series of hastily put up curtains in the hallway outside the main auditorium. It was important though since it allowed us to watch a video playback of the whole routine to see how everything looked on stage.

I watched only half-heartedly, knowing that we had a lot of tough teams in our division. Even without a mistake, I knew there was little chance we were going to come in first place. The thing that I didn't think about, however, was how everyone else on the team would react when they got the news I was anticipating. Or rather the news we were all anticipating. Lexi, Halley, and I even bought bows before awards. Unlike the results announced at the award ceremony, it was my team's reaction to the news that I did not expect.

"Third place never felt so sweet!" Anna announced refusing to take her eyes off of the medal around her neck. It was the same place we got the week before, but since we had no deductions, people were treating it like it had been a first place win.

"It's so shiny!" Halley agreed, turning the medal over to read all the fine print engraved into the reflective circle at the end of a thick blue ribbon.

While the girls around me all went on and on about how excited they were with third, hitting the routine, and also their cool new medals, I once again found myself wanting to leave the competition as soon as possible. The third place medal felt like a participation award they gave out on my kindergarten soccer team. Other people may have been happy with trying a little and getting rewarded for it, but the competitor in me was furious.

"Great job today," Connor said to me, coming over and wrapping his arm around me in a side hug. Much like when he had congratulated me after Blast performed he had a grin plastered on his face. I noticed that he still had his new medal around his neck, bright gold to show Nitro's first place win.

"Thanks," I said weakly, not feeling pleased about coming in third, even if it was out of 7 teams.

"I bet now that everyone is feeling more confident, Nicole will make the routine harder," Connor assured me, clearly picking up on my bad mood.

"I hope so," I sighed. "I just know we can't win Summit unless we get a higher raw score. Not to mention we need to actually hit the harder routine."

"Well, you have three weeks now, which is a whole extra week then I have before Worlds," he reminded me. "I wish you were coming to Worlds, you know. Having you cheering us on would take away some of the stress for sure."

"I tried to get my dad to let me go," I explained with a shrug. "But he said I can't miss two weeks of school in a row. I'll have to settle for Snapchat updates."

Before Connor and I could continue our conversation, Leanne walked over and pulled Connor away from me, something she seemed to be doing more and more of. When he didn't follow her immediately, she tried explaining that she wanted to get a group picture with Connor and some other athletes from their squad with their winning trophy. But, I had a feeling she was just saying it to rub in her first place win since no one else was still taking photos; they had taken so many already just after the awards ceremony. Knowing Leanne always had a motive or a reason that I would never understand, I headed off to find my dad. He was sitting with the other parents, his glittery CHEER DAD shirt standing out like a beacon.

"When are we leaving?" I asked him, slipping off my medal from around my neck and tucking it into my cheer bag sitting at his feet. I also used the chance to pull on my sweatpants over my uniform skirt. Now that awards were over I was allowed to cover up without one of the coaches giving me a warning for not being properly dressed.

"Did Nicole say you were all dismissed?" he asked in reply.

"I don't know," I slowly admitted, instantly knowing what he was going to say next. "I'll go back until we are."

Turning back around, I made my way over to where the rest of the athletes from my gym were all standing and hanging out. The idea of listening to everyone go on and on about winning, or congratulating Blast for coming in third was just making my head start to ache. I knew I had Tylenol in my bag to help with that as needed, but first I needed to wait until Nicole, Tonya, or TJ gave us the okay to head home. Keeping my attention on my phone so I could avoid talking to anyone around me, I didn't even notice Connor was once again standing next to me until he spoke.

"Does this mean you're finally texting me back?"

"Of course," I lied, flashing Connor a nervous smile before shooting him a quick red heart and bow emoji to represent Blast and cheer all at the same time. After sending it, I was happy to look around and see Leanne nowhere in sight.

"You're not a good liar, you know that?" he asked, nudging me with his elbow with a laugh.

"I guess I better practice more," I said, putting on a very serious and determined look. "You're a terrible cheerleader and you'll never win first place again."

"Well, we can't be friends anymore then," he frowned. "Because someone as amazing as you can only have friends who are just as good as you at cheer."

I opened my mouth to reply but didn't get the chance. Instead, Nicole interrupted our conversation by clapping the sequence of claps that I had heard on the first day at the gym before I was even on a team yet. What had once been confusing and strange, was now second nature. I responded by repeating the claps back to Nicole, as did the other athletes around me. Once we stopped clapping it was quiet and Nicole began talking to the group.

"I'm so proud of all of you today!" she beamed. "We brought 7 of our competition teams and 5 are walking away with first, with the other two teams finishing in the top three spots as well. Great job everyone." She paused while everyone cheered. "Some of you will be heading to Worlds in just two weeks, and some of you will be heading to Summit in three weeks. So now, more than ever, it's super important to get some rest. I want all of you to stretch tomorrow and drink lots of water. Practices these next two weeks are going to be really critical, so come to the gym ready to work. I want athletes on Dynamite and Flame to stick around for a second, but the rest of you are dismissed. Go home, get that rest, and we'll see some of you at the gym Monday and Tuesday for everyone else."

Everyone began saying goodbye and giving hugs and taking last minute selfies before walking off in various directions. Those on Dynamite, our senior all girl level 3 team, and Flame, our junior all girl level 2 team, were done performing for the season, so they were giving lots of hugs and even crying. I, on the other hand, turned with little more than a goodbye over my shoulder to Connor and went straight to my dad. He gave me a bit of a frown, but just helped pick up all my gear to leave. Peter and Kyle also helped, and before I knew it, we were loaded into the car. We still had an hour's drive ahead of us, but it was really nice to be out of the high school finally.

"Are you okay?" Peter asked me. He was sitting in the back seat with me for the ride home and looked at me with a bit of concern at the aggressive way I was removing my makeup with a cleansing wipe.

"I guess," I shrugged. "Today just went exactly how I thought it was going to."

"You thought you were going to win third?" he challenged me with a single eyebrow raise.

"No," I began slowly, pausing in removing my makeup. "I thought we were going to place even worse. I guess I just knew walking in we weren't going to come in first. Not with a routine that's so safe and basic."

"Do you have to win? Like, do you only like cheer if you win?"

His question was a little shocking to me, but I knew he wasn't trying to be mean about it. Peter was just asking me an honest question. I thought about it over for a while, wanting to explain it in a way that would make sense to my best friend. Even though I had only known him for three years, living next door to Peter and playing with him and Kyle every day since my dad and I moved in helped me to understand him, and also know how to best pick my words.

"I'm doing something brand new at the gym. I'm the newest person not just on my team, but at the whole gym. So there are some things that are really hard for me. But then there are other things that are really easy for me. And I put in 100% effort every time I go to the gym so I can get better. Like, not just to do what my team needs me to do, but also get better in general. I'm putting in all this work and time and effort, and then I go to practice and watch girls only half trying on everything. They can land these moves if they pushed a little harder or really wanted it. But they don't. They don't seem to really want it that much at all. So I don't feel like putting in the effort on my part is worth it anymore just to watch them fail and be proud they got a shiny participation trophy."

Peter was quiet for a long time. Long enough, in fact, that I was certain he wasn't even listening to me. Then, he just kind of nodded, like it all made sense. It was like he understood exactly what I was going through and just didn't have the words to describe it.

So instead he just nodded, then asked if I wanted to go on a bike ride Sunday afternoon. And, as odd as it sounds, that was another reason why I loved having Peter for a best friend. He didn't feel like he had to change my mind or cheer me up, he just listened and was okay with it all. It helped me feel a little better about my third place medal, knowing I had a first place friend like him.

CHAPTER 7

Pedaling my legs as hard as I could, I raced to the end of the sidewalk, then slid to a stop. I looked back to see Peter and Kyle walking their bikes up the massive hill I had just conquered. My breathing was labored and my legs hurt, but like always, I refused to walk the hill or even take it slow. It was always a fun challenge I made for myself, and after the long day at the cheerleading competition on Saturday it felt nice to really go all out and exert myself.

"One time I'm going to race you and beat you up this hill," Peter said as he finally reached me. As always he was walking his own bike and also holding up Kyle's as well. It was little moments like that when Peter acted like a nice older brother.

"I'll believe it when I see it," I replied, taking off down the street towards the park at the edge of town.

As we pulled up to the park's bike rack, I saw a few kids our age playing tag on the playground equipment and knew we would likely join them. Anytime we came to the park, people were usually playing a community game of one kind or another. But, as we were walking closer, I saw that one of the girls on the play structure was someone I knew.

"Hey Hillary," I called out, walking over to her as she jumped down from her perch on the outside of the tunnel slide.

"Hey, Max," Hillary replied before turning and telling her friends she was taking a time out of the game. When she turned back to me she was giving me a strange look. "Are you wearing makeup?"

"I must not have washed my face all the way," I mumbled, rubbing at my eyes, knowing it was likely some stray eyeliner she caught sight of. Even after the makeup wipes and scrubbing my face before bed, some of my makeup would stay on occasionally. Not to mention I could go a week without cheerleading and still randomly find glitter somewhere on me.

"It's from cheer right?" When I froze she continued. "You've posted pictures about it a lot on Instagram."

"Oh, right," I shrugged, suddenly a little less stressed about needing to explain. Mostly because I knew I also had posted a few videos of my tumbling to my account, one of which Hillary had said was 'epic.'

"So are you going to be at the pitching clinic this week?" Hillary asked, brushing her frizzy brown hair out of her face.

"Wait, what?" I asked immediately, genuinely shocked by her comment.

"The pitching clinic," she said again. She spoke a little slower to make sure I understood. "The first one is this week. You're still playing this year, right?"

I nodded, trying to figure out how I didn't know about the clinics sooner. Sure, I wasn't a pitcher, but as a catcher, it was important that I be there all the same. Coaches for the town's softball league used the clinics to not only find their pitchers but also their catchers, although it was 'just a rumor' if you ever asked any of the coaches. Either way, as someone who played catcher more than any other position, it was my chance to get one step closer to making it onto one of the top teams. In order to do that, I needed to show everyone I was someone worth picking for their team, and the pitching clinic was the perfect place to get that ball rolling. Since it was going to be my first year in an older age division, making an impression on the coaches even before tryouts was super important. But, as all of that ran through my head I realized that my dad and I had never talked about softball for the upcoming season. With cheer filling up my time so much, it was like all other sports took the back burner.

"I'm going to text my dad and see if he got the paperwork for it or anything," I told Hillary as I pulled my cell phone out of my pocket and quickly sent a message. "When is it again?"

"It's Wednesday and Thursday this week, starting at 5. I'd have to check on the other days next week, though. I can't remember them off the top of my head."

"Thanks," I smiled, adding the information in another text I sent my dad's way.

"Are you going to play?" Hillary asked me then, gesturing towards the play structure where Peter and Kyle were playing with the other kids that were there when we arrived.

"Yup," I answered, slipping my phone back into my pocket of my basketball shorts. "What's the game?"

And just like that, I headed over to join in with Hillary and everyone else. We were playing an intense game of grounders, which was a tag style game that involved the tagger closing their eyes when they were on the play structure. It was one we played often, so entering the game was easy enough. It also proved to be quite a distraction until I got home and could talk to my dad about what Hillary had told me.

"What about cheer?" my dad asked as soon as I asked if he had gotten my texts. We were eating dinner on the back deck, a nice spread of pizza and salad that my dad had all set up when I got home from the park.

"Oh," I said simply. I hadn't thought about the fact that the clinic was the same time as Blast practice until that moment. Until then all I could think about was getting a spot on a good softball team.

"I got the paper in the mail a week or two ago," he explained. "It's hanging up on the

75

fridge and everything. I assumed you saw it but weren't interested."

"Really?" I asked.

As if I didn't believe him I stood up and walked inside. Sure enough, the bright yellow flier was front and center on the fridge. It was right next to my gym schedule, an invite for Lexi's birthday party next month, and a photo of my dad and I that Lexi had taken at my first competition of the cheer season. They were things I looked at often, and yet I never paid attention to the bright yellow page. I read it quickly, noticing the dates Hillary couldn't remember. One was a Sunday evening, and another was the day after we were scheduled to fly to Florida for Summit. The conflict I felt was building more and more as I walked out onto the deck to join my dad.

"Was it there?" he asked with a laugh as I sat back down. I nodded. "So I'm guessing this means you want to do softball then?"

"I think so," I shrugged, trying to wrestle with my thoughts. "But if I don't go to the pitching clinics then I won't have a shot at a good team. And if I miss practice right now, so close to Summit, then I have a feeling Nicole and the whole team is going to be really mad at me. Maggie had a fever for a week last month and never missed a single practice or anything. If I miss for something like this then no one is going to be happy. But, since I can't even go to the last clinic since we'll be gone, going to the first few are super important."

"True," he nodded. He took the time to set his silverware down and take a long sip of his iced tea before continuing. "But how will you feel if you miss cheer practice for the clinic?"

"Fine," I said easily. "I don't have any trouble with the routine, and my group never drops stunts. One practice won't suddenly make me a bad cheerleader or something. No one will even notice I'm gone I bet."

"Then there's your answer."

My dad stood up and started cleaning the dinner dishes. I watched him for a minute, not sure what to do or say. It was just a little shocking that he made one comment and then thought it was good enough to just move on. My head was still flying a million miles a second and trying to decide whether or not I could really miss cheer without big consequences.

"But what if Nicole is mad?" I finally asked. As my coach, I knew it was Nicole that was the real person to consider in all of this.

"She might be," he answered as he walked into the kitchen. I followed him, grabbing the remaining dishes from the table. "But I think if you talk it through with her at practice tomorrow then she won't mind too much if you miss one day. I think when you explain to her that softball is important to you, but also explain that you are still committed to cheer, then she'll be okay with you missing the one night."

"That's easier said than done," I said, more to myself than to my dad. But, of course, he heard the comment.

"I know Nicole can be intense at times," he began as he loaded the dishwasher. "But she cares about you girls. And I know she is going to understand. Other girls have other sports they do and things they have outside of the gym. She's not going to be upset for you wanting to think about life after this season of cheer." There was a pause then. "Speaking of which, have you thought more about next season?"

"No," I admitted easily. "I want to just get through Summit first, and then I'll have time to think about it."

"You might want to think about it a little between now and then," he advised, turning to look at me. "If you miss cheer for the pitching clinic and make a good team that might be the start of you needing to miss out on team events. Maybe not right now, but in a few months if you're on a squad at the gym doing practices and conditioning over the summer, doing softball might mean you have to miss time with one of the two sports."

I distracted myself with loading the dishwasher, my head beginning to hurt with all the intense thinking. Nicole was less intimidating to me now then she was when I first joined the gym when she had called me 'Maxine' all the time. But once she learned that only my mom ever called me by my full name, she started calling me Max and it was like the breakthrough in our relationship. After that, I felt more comfortable around her, and she showed me she cared about me and wanted me to learn and grow as a cheerleader. But, out of the three owners, she was the person I was least excited to have a conversation with about missing cheer. Telling Tonya or even TJ would be a little less nerve-wracking. Tonya and I were super close thanks to some bonding moments when I started at the gym. TJ, even though I didn't know him super well, seemed to always be laughing and joking, so he was clearly pretty easy going. None of that mattered, though. I would need to talk to Nicole to get out of Thursday night's cheer practice, and I was already dreading it.

CHAPTER 8

"Straight legs and you got this," Halley said to me as she placed her hands on my back to help toss me into the air. It was the same reminder she gave me every time I was about to do my full around. Sometimes I wondered if it really made a difference, but since I always made sure to keep my legs extra straight in the move, I had a feeling it might have helped at least a little.

As I landed back in the arms of my stunt team after the sing around, Anna told me her usual, "Awesome Max," as I announced "Good catch." It was all as much a part of the routine as everything else we did on the mat. Between every skill or jump or tumbling pass, we were always calling out things like that to one another. The added encouragement and 'mat talk' as Nicole called it, helped us to stay focused on what we were doing and also to break down the routine and take it one thing at a time.

Unfortunately, the mat talk was doing little to keep stunts in the air. After everything hit at the competition, Nicole wanted us to try the same routine a few times. That was a great way to start practice. But, since we hit everything, she wanted us to add back in a few changes that we had taken out less than a week ago. And that, as I feared it would, caused girls to no longer stay in the air on their flying. Tumbling passes were more or less hitting as planned, but without harder flying, I knew winning at Summit was next to impossible.

"Get some water. We're going to work on pyramid for a bit before we try everything full out again."

At Nicole's instruction, we all walked to our bags and grabbed our water bottles. I looked around and saw a few girls lying down on the mats to rest, or sitting down to stretch.

A lot of people were struggling after the practice, and it wasn't even over yet. Taking a long drink of my water I realized that it was a great time to talk to Nicole. Not that I was looking forward to that moment. Thankfully Lexi walked over and distracted me so I could put off talking about softball a little longer.

"You hit the scorpion, right?" Lexi asked me, a determined look on her face.

"Of course," I nodded, knowing Lexi and I were the only two that managed to stay in the air on the move after Nicole added it back in at the start of the team practice.

"Perfect," she grinned, taking a drink from her water bottle before turning to walk off again.

"Lexi," I called to her, making her turn to face me. "What are you doing?"

"I had an idea," she said quickly, pulling on my arm so I was forced to take a few steps away from the rest of the girls around us. "If Nicole will let us still pull the move, we can change the timing on when the other girls go up so it looks like we were the only ones that were ever going to do it."

"But won't it look weird with me on the far left and you at center?" I asked, knowing that spacing and position on the mat was just as important as the skills we were performing.

"We would have to rearrange a little, but I think it could work to bring our routine up to the level where we need to be," she grinned. "What do you think?"

"I like it," I said honestly. "But would Nicole really be willing to make that change?"

"I'm about to go find out."

Then Lexi walked off towards Nicole who was talking to Tonya. It was clear from their facial expressions that they were a little stressed about the routine. Taking out a lot of the harder skills was okay for one competition, but adding them back in was apparently the plan all along. Now that they were trying to add even more of the skills back in without success, it was clear they were working on a new strategy. Sure, we still had three weeks to get ready for Summit, but that time was ticking away quickly.

Trying not to stress about it too much, I sat down and worked on stretching. I didn't need to stretch to do any of the moves I performed on the mat with Blast, but I knew I would be glad for the extra stretching Friday as I worked on more stunting with Connor and Gwen and everyone else. Thinking about working on skills with them without really knowing if I was going to be coming back to the gym for another season or not was strange. Since my dad brought it up to me I had been stressing about it a lot. I knew I had a little time to think about it, and hopefully there would be a chance at Summit for me to even talk it over with some of the girls on the team. Staying at the gym would be an easier decision if I knew I was going to be able to be on a team with a lot of the girls I had gotten to know all season. Or had their support if I was choosing to leave for softball.

"Gather around ladies," Nicole called out, stopping me in my stretches. As I stood up and headed towards her, Lexi came sprinting my way with a skip in her step.

"She agreed?" I asked Lexi, although I more or less knew the answer thanks to the ear to ear smile on her face. But before she could answer me, Nicole began talking again.

"Okay everyone, we're going to do something a little different," Nicole began, a much less stressed look on her face than just minutes before. "You ladies are pushing hard and doing your best, but we have some skills right now that are a little less than consistent. So we're going to go back to the same flying we did this past weekend. The new tumbling we added to help up our raw score is going to stay for now, and then Thursday we are going to rework some of the elite flying sections so we can be on track to hopefully make the finals at Summit. We're going to spend the rest of tonight running the pyramid just like we did it last weekend, and then work on the new tumbling. But Thursday everyone needs to come to the gym ready to work hard. We have some bigger changes to make for most of the stunt teams, so it's going to be a long night. Let's set up for pyramid and end the night on a good note."

Her words left me reeling. I spend the next 45 minutes working on pyramid, tumbling, and trying to figure out how I was going to tell Nicole I wasn't going to be there Thursday. At the start of practice, it seemed like a hard conversation to have. But, after hearing how important the next team practice was going to be, it had me doubting if I really should go to the pitching clinic at all. As I finally walked up to Nicole at the end of the night though, I wasn't sure if I was even going to be able to get all of the words out.

"Nicole, can I talk to you for a second?" I asked before I lost the nerve.

"Of course," Nicole smiled back at me. "What is it, Max?"

"Well, um, I wanted to tell you something." It was a weak start, but I kept going just so I could be done with it. "I have a softball clinic I need to go to on Thursday so I won't be at practice. I would have told you sooner but I just found out about it yesterday, and I need to go if I want to make it onto a good team for the season."

There was a pause after I spoke, as Nicole tried to take everything in. It felt like a million years went by in that time, but it was actually only a few seconds. That was a good thing too since I held my breath the whole time.

"We're making a lot of changes on Thursday that involve you and Lexi primarily," she slowly told me. "Are you sure if you miss it you will be about to catch up on everything?"

"I think so," I nodded. "I never really struggled with the old routine, so even if we change everything back to that I think I'll be okay."

"That's very true." Nicole glanced over at the other girls of Blast as they were packing up their gear, and then back at me. "Max, do you like cheerleading?"

"Of course," I replied, not really sure where that question had come from.

"Is it just because it's so easy for you?"

"No," I said with a shake of my head. "I like that I got to make friends and work on some harder stuff sometimes too."

"But nothing we've been doing on Blast has been hard for you for a long time now." Even though Nicole's statement was a fact, it also sounded a little like a question. I more or less just shrugged in response, not sure what else to do or say. "You're an amazing cheerleader. And the gym is lucky to have you here. But I think we're not challenging you enough. Next year we want you to move to one of our senior teams, as long as you're interested."

"Really?" Her comment made sense after all of my time in skills classes, but it was still a little weird to hear. Moving up to a level 4 team was one thing, but until that moment I always assumed any move I made would be to another junior team.

"Absolutely," Nicole said with a smile. "You're really talented, and we know you have even more potential than we've seen so far. But I don't think any of that matters if it's not what you want. I'm not saying you missing a practice means you're quitting the gym. But I want you to really think about how much cheerleading means to you. If you make a senior team, then missing practice for things like softball clinics won't be something that can happen often."

"I understand," I said as seriously as I could. I was glad my dad had mentioned almost the same thing so I had already been mulling it over some time. "Right now I just don't feel like missing one day is going to matter much. The skills are easy enough for me that sometimes practice feels like I can just be going through the motions and still make everything hit."

"You aren't being challenged at Blast." Nicole's way of summing it up was perfect. She said it with a serious look on her face, one I didn't know how to interpret. "Well, best of luck at the softball clinic. When you're here Friday for your skills class I will fill you in a little on everything and then next Monday you can get everything under your belt. If you and your stunt group can make it Saturday to the open gym that would be a good time to play catch up as well."

"Okay," I replied with my best attempt at a smile. "Thanks, Nicole."

I walked over and grabbed my cheer bag then, not really focusing on the girls around me. Nicole's words were replaying in my mind, and the idea of being on a senior team was almost too much to accept. Part of it was because I knew usually only athletes that were 13 and up got places on senior level teams, despite the fact that 12-year-olds were allowed in that division as well. That fact meant that Lexi, who was only 11, and Halley, who was only 12, would likely not be placed on a team with me. In fact, I realized as I walked towards the door of the gym, there were only three other girls on my squad who were 13. It meant if I stayed at the gym I might be moved to a team where I didn't know anyone at all. The idea of having to start over and getting to know up to 29 other cheerleaders while working on harder skills was intimidating, to say the least. I tried to remind myself that it was only an obstacle I would tackle if I stayed at the gym. And with that decision still up in the air, I tried not to focus on it. Instead, I began focusing on the softball clinics that were now only two days away.

CHAPTER 9

After spending so many months at TNT Force, walking into the middle school gymnasium where the softball pitching clinic was being held was a little strange. First of all, no one was wearing makeup, glittery clothing, or cheer bows. Second of all, it was so serious. Usually, when I arrived at cheerleading practice, I was greeted with hugs and high-fives, people would be laughing and chatting, and everyone was usually smiling and glad to be there. At softball, however, people looked really focused and intense, and not very welcoming at all.

I saw a few girls I kind of recognized as I walked in and headed over to the check-in table. It was a little weird to not have my dad there, but unlike cheerleading, softball wasn't really a sport where parents stayed to watch practice. So, I signed in, pinned a white square of paper with the number 12 on my shirt and then went to get some catching gear on. There was a large group of girls all there to pitch as well as catch, so I quickly slipped on my leg and chest guards and grabbed a face mask so I was ready to go as soon as someone needed me. I assumed I would be able to chat with some of the girls and hang out before we got to work like I was so used to doing at cheer. Unfortunately, that was the complete opposite of how things went.

Instead of chatting and making friends, I was more or less ignored by everyone as they focused on the task at hand. Everyone was there to show their skills, although the clinic was supposed to be a time to work on your pitching with the help of local coaches. The girls in the gymnasium were trying their hardest to throw nice and accurate, to make their pitching appear effortless, and prove they should be on one of the top teams. None of that involved talking to anyone else or getting to know people at all apparently. Some girls seemed to be talking in little groups, but they usually were wearing the same shirt, showing they were on the same team the year before. Although I had played every season since I moved to Texas, it had always been in the younger age division. So, not many people at the clinic would even recognize me. I tried to remind myself of this, thinking it would be different if I knew the other girls walking in. That wasn't too important, though. The important thing was for me to focus on catching and show the coaches what I could do. All I had to do was find someone to team up with that I could catch for.

"I'm Max," I said with a smile as I put my hand out to greet a pitcher who was standing closest to the catching gear pile. "Do you want to work together?"

"I'm Zoe," she said back to me, not shaking my hand. Instead, she looked down at me, her intense brown eyes looking me over. "You're kind of short. Are you sure you can give a good strike zone?"

"Of course," I assured her, knowing that where I held my mit while catching was super important to whoever was pitching. "I've been catching for two years, so I know how to make my height work to my advantage."

"Whatever," Zoe replied, then walked over to one of the open lanes. I shrugged it off, happy to be getting started if nothing else.

The large gym was taped off with blue painter's tape, making it clear where each pitching and catching team should stand. There was a standing coach at each of the lanes, but over time they rotated through to see all of the girls and give tips as needed. Zoe turned out to be a really bad pitcher, throwing wild pitches that I had to struggle to get control of. But, as I had assured her, my experience made me good at my job. Since I was shorter than most of the girls, I was able to shuffle my body easily and only allowed a few balls to get past me.

Eventually, Zoe took a break and I began catching for another girl that was waiting for a turn to pitch. The girl jogged over to my lane as soon as Zoe walked away, clearly eager to show the coaches what she could do. I was hoping to take a little break, but thankfully the new pitcher was a lot better than Zoe. In fact, by the time she was done throwing a few dozen balls my way, I only had to move to catch a few stray throws. She pitched right on the money almost every time.

"You've got a great arm," I told the girl as we were packing up. It was the first time I spoke to her the whole night since I was usually 30 feet away from her. "I'm Max."

"Thanks," she replied with a smile. "I'm Cate. You're really good at catching. That girl throwing before me really made you work for the ball."

"Yeah, just a little," I laughed, glad I was talking to someone who was finally at least a little friendly. "So how long have you been pitching?"

"Just a year," she explained. "But my dad is a baseball coach so I spent a lot of time practicing at home this winter. He coaches my brothers' team so he wanted me to come today so other people could see me pitch too."

"Well, it paid off for sure," I nodded. "I bet you make a good team."

"I hope so," she said with a suddenly nervous look. "I'm not very good at batting, so I'm hoping my pitching will make up for it."

"I bet it will," I quickly assured her. We were walking together as we chatted, heading outside to where parents and cars were waiting. I spotted my dad easily. "See you tomorrow?"

"Yup, see you then," Cate said with a wave.

Climbing into my dad's car I was immediately grilled on how the clinic had gone. My dad must have been getting used to watching at TNT Force, so not knowing how things went was a little stressful for him. I assured him everything went great, leaving out the fact that no one but Cate seemed all that interested in getting to know me. I'm not sure why I didn't tell him about Zoe or the other girls, but in that moment it felt like it would make the idea of missing cheer practice the next night unnecessary. Besides, I was at the clinic to showcase my catching, not to make friends. I could focus on that once I was actually placed on a team in a few more weeks.

Less than 24 hours later, I was back at the middle school gymnasium, and once again catching for Cate. I noticed a lot fewer girls were in attendance for the second night, including Zoe who likely realized she wasn't as good at pitching as she thought before coming to the clinic. The girls that were there, however, still showed no interest in getting to know me. Thankfully Cate was nice enough to make up for it. I was getting used to her throwing and even tried to give her encouragements as I threw the ball back her way. She would also thank me for catching a wild pitch if she threw one, or apologize if she threw one I didn't manage to get ahold of. They were few and far between, so we got a lot of pitching in before the night was over. It also looked like the coaches were taking note of her, and hopefully me. When they stood at our lane near Cate, they didn't give her much advice. Instead they pretty much just watched her pitching with a smile on their face.

"I really hope we make the same team," Cate told me at the end of the clinic on Thursday. We were taking off our numbers and leaving them at the table for the next pitching clinic as well as the softball tryouts that were in a few weeks.

"That would be awesome," I agreed honestly. "Hopefully it's on a really good team too. I took this year off of basketball so I'm really hoping getting on the right team for softball will make up for it."

"Why did you take basketball off?"

As soon as the question was out of Cate's mouth I knew I shouldn't have said anything. It was like I was suddenly afraid to let her know I did cheerleading. Not because it wasn't something I enjoyed, but because she looked like someone who felt about cheerleading how I did before I joined the gym. Almost exactly in fact. She had on loose gray shorts and a t-shirt for a BBQ restaurant across town. Her dirty blonde hair was in a super messy bun, and I got the feeling she never wore makeup or glitter. So, for a second I worried what she might think if she knew about my time at the TNT Force form. But, worried or not, in that moment I knew I had to tell the truth. Cate was the only person who was nice enough to even talk to me, so lying to her about something that filled so much of my life didn't seem very friendly.

"I'm on an all star cheerleading team," I explained quickly. "I would have had to miss a lot of competitions to do basketball, and since I'm not getting any taller I thought maybe skipping a season would be a good idea."

"Cheerleading? Like, for your school?" Cate asked, her eyes narrowing slightly.

"Not really," I said with a shake of my head. "It's an all star team. We compete at big arenas most weekends, and my team is actually a really high ranked team in the country. There are people on the team who travel an hour one way just to be a part of the gym."

"Oh, cool," she said, although I noticed she wasn't really looking at me much anymore. It was weird, but it was as if the mention of cheerleading had her instantly less interested in chatting with me.

"Well, see you at the next clinic," I said, hoping to catch her eye, but she ignored me to check her phone.

In response Cate just nodded, leaving me to walk to the car by myself. I walked slowly, trying to make sure I understood what had just happened. Did Cate really just brush me off once she found out I did cheer? I was hoping it was just my imagination, or me making a big deal out of nothing. Putting on a smile when I climbed into my dad's car, I pulled out my phone and was shocked to see I had over a dozen missed messages. It was just what I needed to take my mind off of the strange interaction with Cate.

CHAPTER 10

My thumbs were sore from texting before I could convince all of my friends to calm down. I had to assure them over and over again that I was just at the softball clinic for the evening and that I was coming back to the gym Friday for my skills class and again Saturday for the open gym time. They went on and on asking me if I was leaving the gym for good, if I didn't tell them because I was upset at them, and then to let me know if I needed someone to talk to about anything, they were there for me. Okay, that last one was only from Lexi and Halley, but I had the feeling it was generally implied all around. I assured everyone I was only missing the one practice, that I would be back in the gym soon, and that everything was okay.

The only problem was that everything was not okay. The way Cate brushed me off had me confused, to say the least. Would anyone else at softball have a problem with the fact I was also a cheerleader? Would being a part of the TNT Force gym keep me from getting on a good team, or even making friends at softball? The stress of worrying and overthinking all of it made me less and less excited for Summit. I knew I was going to have to learn new parts of the Blast routine that I missed at Thursday's night practice, and on top of that, I knew that after the busy weekend at the gym, it was sure to be another week of long practices as well. Walking into the cheer gym, unlike when I entered the gymnasium for the pitching clinic, I was thankfully welcomed with open arms. Literally. As I entered the TNT Force building for my skills class on Friday night, Connor was waiting for me at the door and pulled me into a massive hug. It was like until I actually arrived at the gym, people were at kind of worried I was really gone for good after missing the one night.

"I'm glad you're here," he said to me. He had heard about me missing practice from Lexi when she texted him and Gwen to see if they knew where I was. Apparently, I learned as the texts came in, Nicole didn't tell the team I was out for a softball clinic. It caused quite a bit of unnecessary panic, but hopefully, that was more or less behind us.

"I'm glad I'm here too," I said as I stepped back from the hug. "Did you think I wasn't going to be here?"

"No," he finally replied. "I just don't think I say it enough and wanted to make sure I let you know."

Before I could say anything in reply, Gwen came over and gave me the most awkward hug she could think of. She stood next to me and wrapped her arms around my body at my shoulders, squeezing me way too tight while she smashed her face into my hair and pretended to cry. I was struggling to get away while I laughed at her antics at the same time.

"Enough of that," Michael said with a laugh. "Sorry if my sister was on a rampage last night Max."

"Lexi?" I asked although I knew it was his only sister. "She was just making sure I didn't do something crazy without telling her."

"You mean Lexi was overreacting?" Connor asked with a pretend shocked look on his face. "Never!"

"Hey, you messaged me last night too," I reminded him, giving his arm a push for emphasis.

We joked around for a little while longer. Then it was time to get to work. Greg was there to help us work on tumbling a little bit, but the main focus of the evening was to pick up where we left off the last time we were all together. This meant that I was held up by everyone one at a time, so they could work on their grips while I was in the air doing various flying poses. As always, I felt weird to only have two hands holding me up, but I was getting more used to it. It was also hard since each person that was stunting under me did things just a little different. Gwen and Connor, who were the newest ones to stunting like that, were having a hard time. To give them a break, after a lot of failed attempts, we eventually moved on to some other stunts as well.

"We're going to work on an inversion double up," Tonya explained after we did some basic cupie and liberty poses. "This is a two-man stunt, so let's start with Reid and Michael."

"Thanks," Gwen said, pretending to be offended.

"You're next," Tonya replied, going to stand between Reid and Michael.

The great thing about working with Tonya was that she could not only teach flying, she could also still fly. So, she went over how the guys would need to hold her, explained to me where to put my hands and how to hold my body position, but then she actually did the whole stunt. Tonya began to do a handstand, but before she could get all the way vertical, Reid and Michael grabbed onto her where she had shown them. They held her torso and legs so they would be ready for the next portion of the stunt. Tonya counted out loud, then pushed off the ground with her hands as the boys lifted her up until she was standing above their heads with her feet supported under her. They spun her around twice on the way to getting her vertical, making it a difficult level 5 stunt. But of course, she managed to make it look effortless as usual.

As the boys brought her back down to the ground I could see they were unaffected by flying Tonya instead of myself. The was likely because Tonya was only a few inches taller than me, and skinny despite her muscles. She had short cropped wavy brown hair, light hazel eyes, and always had on enough makeup to look put together but not overdone. Basically, she still looked like a cheerleader, just a little bit more grown up. And really, that was the perfect way to describe all three of the owners of TNT Force. After a month or two at the gym, I learned from Halley that the three of them were on a college cheer team and after they graduated decided they wanted to open their own gym. So, they created TNT Force, using the first letter of their names for inspiration. That was 6 years ago, and based on the move Tonya had just done, it was clear that cheerleading was still her passion.

"You ready to try it?" Tonya asked once she was safely on the ground.

"I think so," I said and went to work.

It was a little harder than how it looked when Tonya did the skill, mostly because it was a move that Michael, Reid, and Tonya had done a few times before, even if it wasn't all together. After all, Michael was on Nitro, and Reid was a member of Detonators, both senior level 5 teams. I sometimes got the feeling they were there mostly to help out when new moves were harder to learn for

Connor and Gwen, but I knew it also helped them get in extra practice on their stunting. We tried the new skill a few times with only one twist on my way up, but added the second one in soon enough. Once we got the stunt looking more or less how it should, Gwen and Connor had their chance to try it. Connor was on Nitro, and it was only his first year on the level 5 team. Gwen, on the other hand, had been on Bomb Squad for two years but was still learning the harder base work. So, with them under me, I fell a few times before I got up with only one twist. Before I knew it though, they had me in the air as well.

"So now are you ready to try it with a tick tock heel stretch?" Tonya asked after both pairs worked on the skill a little more.

"Let's do it!" I announced quickly. Although everyone was tired, I was the only one who had slammed onto the mats a few times. So, if I was good to be picked up and tossed, I knew everyone else was likely ready to go again as well.

First with Reid and Matthew, and then again with Connor and Gwen, I was lifted into the air from the handstand position and then spun around two times before they held me upright. But then, as soon as I was more or less stable I held one foot up next to my head.

Then, in one swift movement, I traded the foot that was in the air with the foot that was being held up, so it was now my left foot I was holding up instead of the right. The move was difficult even without the spins leading into it, so I naturally came out of the air a few more times before we landed it with each group. Then we called it a night with the flying. Everyone else spent a little time tumbling, but my body was not feeling great after the number of times I landed on the mats or the people below me, so I allowed myself a bit of a break.

"I think I'm going to have a bruise from that last one," I idly complained as I sat stretching my right arm after we were done with the practice. Reid and Matthew were still working on a tumbling pass, but Gwen sat with me on the side of the blue mat where we had been practicing. Across the gym, Fuze, the purple team, were warming up for their nightly practice.

"Do you need some ice for that?" Gwen asked, looking at the purple and red mark that was blooming on the inside of my upper arm.

"I think I have some Icy Hot in my cheer bag," I said with a shrug. "I'm not too worried about it though. At least if it's still there by Summit my uniform will cover it."

"Spoken like a true cheerleader," Gwen laughed.

"Well, if the bruises fit," I laughed as well, holding up my right arm for emphasis.

Gwen and I sat chatting for a few more minutes, but when my dad came out of the viewing room and made a big show of looking at his watch, it was clear I needed to take off. He was eager to get home since he was recording something on The Discovery channel, so I said a quick goodbye and followed him out the door. It wasn't until I was in the car that I even thought again about how things had gone at the pitching clinic. I remembered the girls not really getting to know me at softball, and it made me think about when I first joined the TNT Force gym. It dawned on me in that moment that maybe I was the one not giving them a chance. I made a mental note to try to be more outgoing when I was at the next clinic in just over a week. But, before then, I had a lot to worry about. Well, really just the open gym, but as I sat stretching, it felt like a lot. My muscles were sore enough that the thought of practice made me even more exhausted. But I knew my friends would be excited to see me and teach me the new changes to the Blast routine for

Summit. That helped to level out my overall mood. At least a little.

CHAPTER 11

Walking into the TNT Force gym on Saturday morning, I was struck with a sense of déjà vu. It had been an open gym session that I attended in August where I first met the coaches and learned about what joining the cheer gym would be like. Back then I was certain I was never going to do cheerleading or act like the girls I saw that day wearing shiny bows and smiling bigger than cartoon characters. But, things had changed a lot in just a few months. Sure, I didn't wear a lot of the shiny and glittery clothing when I wasn't in uniform. But, unlike that first day, I no longer walked into the gym and felt out of place. Instead, I was instantly mobbed by my friends; I'm sure they were still a little worried they might never see me at the cheerleading gym ever again.

"We have to teach you so many things from practice," Halley said to me while Lexi was going on and on about the new place I would be standing on the mat before my stunts.

"You don't go left anymore, since that's where Kenzie is," Lexi said, oblivious to Halley talking to me at the same time.

"Slow down," I laughed, finally getting them both to stop talking. "How about you guys talk me through it on the mat and then we can start trying stuff if we want."

With a nod, both girls led me over to the open mat where only a few people were working on tumbling. As long as we kept an eye on them it was easy enough to stay out of the way and avoid any collisions. The two girls, along with Anna, Olivia, and Skyler from my stunt team walked me through the changes and then let me try everything once or twice. It was easy enough to learn, and when we were done I was pretty certain I would be able to learn it all fast enough. This was mostly because a lot of the moves were ones we had in before we watered down the routine. I knew adding them back in would help, but in the back of my head I had a feeling making it to the final at Summit, let alone winning, was not going to be as easy as we thought back when we got the Summit bid at the start of the season.

"Do you want to try it all again?" Halley asked after we sat for a few minutes to rest after running everything a few times.

"Yeah, I just need some water," I explained, standing up and walking towards where my cheer bag was waiting.

As I looked across the room I saw a lot of now familiar faces working on various skills on the blue mats. Spotting Connor I gave him a wave then grabbed my water. But, before I could even take a sip I heard someone calling out my name. Glancing to where it was coming from, I saw that Nicole was heading my way.

"Great job on the changes," Nicole said, nodding to the mat where my friends were waiting for me. "Do you have a minute to chat in the office?"

"Thanks, and yeah I can chat," I replied, already nervous for some reason.

I glanced back and held up one finger to my friends to let them know I would be back in a minute, then followed after Nicole. She walked us to the offices near the gym entrance. When I entered Nicole's small office I was confused to see my dad sitting on the couch instead of in the viewing room with the other parents. But when he patted the seat next to him I instantly walked over and sat down. Turning back to Nicole I saw she was smiling but also had a very serious look on her face. It did little to ease my growing nerves.

"How did the softball clinic go?" Nicole asked, sitting in an armchair that was more or less across from where I was sitting with my dad.

"Good," I said evenly. "I have another clinic next weekend, so it will be another chance for some coaches to see me in action." I didn't even mention the clinic that would happen while I was in Florida for Summit, knowing it was something I could never miss.

"Well that's great," Nicole nodded. "I think softball will be a great way to get some extra conditioning in over the summer."

I didn't know what to say to Nicole, so I just smiled weakly. I had a feeling she didn't ask me to come sit in the office with my dad just to talk about softball. But, at that moment,

I had no idea what the real reason could be. Being patient right now was not easy.

"I've been thinking since our chat at Blast practice Tuesday night that it would be great for you to have a chance to really push yourself as an athlete here at the gym," Nicole began, finally getting around to the point. "The skills class is great, but it's different when you're actually performing. I talked to some of the other coaches, and we were brainstorming some ideas, but we weren't really sure what could possibly be done so late in the season. Well, until last night. You left right after your skills class didn't you?"

"Yeah. I think it was around 6:30."

"That's what I thought," Nicole paused for a second. "I don't suppose anyone told you about Cassidy then."

"No," I replied, although as I said it I realized it sounded more like a question.

"She fell yesterday," Nicole frowned. Her tone was sincere as she described what happened, and I knew it must have been hard as a coach to watch someone get hurt. "We were running Fuze's routine towards the end of practice and Cassidy was doing her elite flying section like always. She always hits it in practice and had never even bobbled it at competition. But last night something went wrong and she fell out of the stunt. Her stunt team tried to catch her, but the way she was falling was odd. She pretty much fell sideways over the top of her side base and right onto the ground. The impact broke her collarbone."

My mouth was actually hanging open in shock at Nicole's story. Sprained ankles and even wrists were common enough in the gym, and I saw a lot of athletes wear braces or wrap their injuries while performing. But to hear that someone not only broke a bone but broke it while falling out of the air was as shocking as it was scary.

"Will she be okay?" I asked, trying to imagine the pain of both landing on the ground and also breaking a bone. I had fallen a good number of times, but other than bruises I always walked away fine.

"Her doctor doesn't think she will need surgery. But she will be in a sling for the next few weeks, and then can only start basic exercises through most of the summer. Not to mention the injury is proving to be super painful and has her basically immobile until the swelling can go down and everything can start to heal." The serious look was back on Nicole's face as she continued. "Since Fuze got a bid to Summit we need to either fill her spot or run the routine with one less flyer. And after talking it through with some of the girls last night, and then the other coaches in the gym, we had another idea. We want to ask you to fill her spot in the routine."

"You want me to quit Blast to cheer on Fuze?" I asked, not sure I could believe what I was hearing.

"No, not quit," Nicole quickly corrected me. "Since Blast is a junior level 3, you can crossover to a senior level 4 at Summit and compete on both teams. It would mean learning a new routine rather fast, but we all agreed that you are the best person to fill in the spot on such short notice. You have so much talent and potential, and this is a great way to showcase it best."

I turned and looked at my dad then, my head filled with too many thoughts for my mouth to really understand how to reply. He had a smile on his face and didn't look all that shocked. Clearly, Nicole had already talked to him about everything, likely when he first dropped me off at the gym in the morning for the start of the open gym. Or possibly even on the phone last night. I had learned a long time ago that my dad was just as invested in my life at the gym as any of the cheer moms that spend their evenings in the parent viewing room.

"It's going to be a lot of work," Nicole continued. "You would only have two weeks to learn the routine and get used to performing with a new stunt group. But, we were hoping it would help everyone out. The team could still perform at their highest potential at Summit, and you can experience what performing on a senior team would be like. Next season we want you to be able to move up to a senior team, so this would be a great chance for you to give it a little test run."

"But I would still be on Blast with all of my friends and get to compete with them?" I asked. It was funny that I hadn't been looking forward to Summit all that much in the last week, but suddenly the idea of not getting to perform with my friends and team was a deal breaker.

"Absolutely," she reassured me. "Fuze practices in the later time slot on Tuesday and then again on Friday so you can still go to all of the normal Blast practice like usual. The only thing you might have to miss is your skills class. Greg and Tonya already said they can either move it or just skip the next few weeks so you can focus on everything else. Learning the new routine is going to take some time, and we don't have much of it to spare right now."

"What if I can't learn it all in time?" I finally asked, remembering back to my dance performance during cheer camp in August. For the exercise, I was placed in a group of other fliers from the gym and we were given the task of making up a dance to perform for the whole gym. I was the weak link on the team and the other girls were less than thrilled about it. Leanna, who I had only met once before the dance challenge, seemed to dislike me even more ever since I froze during the routine onstage.

"If you can't learn certain things we will simplify it," Nicole began with a smile. "We can put you in the back for the dance, and you can fake the harder skills so we still get most of the points for it. It's a lot of the same skills you are already doing on Blast, just with a little bit more flying and some harder tumbling. You still won't get to throw fulls, but you will get to do whips instead of just back tucks."

"Okay," I said quietly after a pause that seemed to stretch on forever.

"Okay?" Nicole asked in reply.

"Yeah," I nodded. "I'll give it a try."

And with that, my dad gave me a pat on the shoulder, Nicole gave me a hug, and I went back into the gym to tell my friends the news. I did everything while in a quiet shock, not sure if I was making the right decision at all. Just days before I wasn't sure if I was going to keep cheering after the season was over, and I certainly wasn't looking forward to how sub-par performing at Summit was looking to be with Blast. But then all of a sudden, there I was, on not just one but two teams heading to the last and most important competition of the year. I thought about pinching myself to see if it was all real, but had too much to catch up on to take a break or do anything other than cheer!

CHAPTER 12

Sunday night I sat in my room, doing the unthinkable. I was practicing my cheer hair and makeup while carrying on a snapchat conversation with Lexi and Halley. It was strange, to say the least, but things like that were becoming more and more common for me. What wasn't so common was that instead of the bright red glitter, I was layering a bold purple glitter coat on top of the silver shimmery eyeshadow I was wearing. Before I left the gym Nicole gave me a new makeup bag, letting me know I would get more Fuze team gear later. I wondered if one day I would buy my own makeup like the other girls on my team. Based on the aisles of choices I saw in the stores I was glad that the gym offered kits in the team store that covered all the basics specific to each team color and skin tone.

"PERFECT!" Lexi wrote in a snapchat she sent me where she was holding her thumb up in support. I got a similar message from Halley, only hers was taken with her dog in the photo as if Truffles was also happy with my makeup. I thought about trying to take my own photo with Thunder and Storm, but the kittens were curled up asleep on the end of my bed so I left them alone.

"How am I going to switch?" I sent my friends, complete with a photo of me holding the red and purple glitter up for the camera. It was one of the many things that was causing me stress since accepting Nicole's offer to join a second squad.

After telling Nicole I was going to join Fuze for Summit, I let my friends know the news right away. They were all happy for me, jumping around and screaming so much that Connor came over to make sure no one had died. When I told him the good news he was so happy for me he practically broke me in half with a massive hug. Their excitement had me feeling better about the decision right away.

But, the excitement started to fade as I began to think through the reality of what being on two squads was going to mean.

First of all, I was going to be spending even more time at the gym. This was a small thing, but something that came to mind all the same. The second thing that I realized was that I was going to have to compete up to 5 times at Summit. Since Blast only got a partial bid, we were going to be performing on Friday to see if we made it to the next round. If we did that, then I would have to perform once with each team on Saturday, and then possibly another two times on Sunday if both squads made it to the final. That stress was only intensified when I realized I would need to change my uniform, bow, and makeup between the routines as well.

"BOO!" a voice said from my doorway, making me jump a little. Looking up I was happy to see it was only Peter.

"You scared me," I told him with a laugh as he sat down on my bed and pulled Storm into his lap. Storm looked around for a second, let out a big yawn, then went right back to sleep complete with an extra loud purr.

"You sure are wearing a lot of makeup for someone just hanging out at home," Peter pointed out while gently petting the kitten in his lap.

"I'm trying to practice taking off the purple and putting on the red and then back again," I explained, pointing to the small containers of glitter sitting on my bed. There were also flakes of the glitter all over my blankets, but I was more or less used to that after the month of wearing glittery uniforms and practice wear. Despite being attached to the fabric, glitter had a way of staying on any surface for weeks on end!

"Why?" he asked, his eyes squinting in confusion and likely judgment.

"I'm on another cheer squad," I said simply. I shrugged then began to pack up all of my makeup that was lying out in front of me. "Nicole asked me to join a level 4 team for Summit, so I have to get used to performing on two teams and everything that goes with it. Hopefully, she will let me just wear one glitter color all day or something because this is going to be super hard to take off and put back on so quickly."

"Hold on," Peter stopped me. "What do you mean you're on another squad?"

"I'm on two teams now," I explained. "The same team I've been on, and then the purple team. Someone got hurt so I'm filling her spot so the teams still have a shot at the finals for Summit."

"And you're okay with that?" he asked. "Weren't you thinking about being done with cheer for good just yesterday morning?"

Until he said those words I had almost forgotten about our lunch conversation the day before. After we went swimming all morning with Kyle, the three of us sat on my deck eating lunch before I headed to the gym. Kyle was distracted making his dinosaur chicken nuggets attack one another, but Peter was asking me how the pitching clinic had gone. When I told him how great it was and the fact that I was thinking I had a shot at a good team after catching for two people at the clinic, Peter was confused. Until I actually went through with the clinic he assumed that I was going to skip the softball season just like I had skipped basketball. Not able to hide anything from my best friend, I admitted to him then that I wasn't sure if I was going to be heading back to cheerleading for another season. This was mostly since the idea of not being on a team with my friends, or at least not on a winning team with my friends, was less than appealing.

Little did I know I was going to go to the gym that same day and get asked to join a second team where I could learn harder skills and also possibly make even more friends. Instead, I talked with Peter honestly and openly that day about my frustrations at being on a team that wasn't going to win. Not to mention the fact that I wasn't loving that no one else on my team seemed ready to put in the work to really get better at skills. Peter listened to everything, allowed me to vent at times, and then when I was all done he basically told me that he would feel the same way if he was in my shoes. So, as he sat there on my bed looking at me with confusion after hearing I was suddenly on not just one but two cheerleading squads, I felt like I should have told him sooner.

"I wanted to quit," I told him, busying myself with reaching past him to pick up Thunder and setting him on my lap. Petting his soft fur was a nice bit of added comfort as I explained the rather stressful situation I found myself facing. "I kind of figured I was going to just end out the season, then not show up at the tryouts and move on. But when Nicole was talking to me about joining the new team she was telling me that the reason they wanted me to do it was because they want me to be on a senior team next year. They want me to finally be on a team that is more my skill level."

"But why aren't you on one of those teams now? Or why can't people on your team actually try?"

"I don't know," I said finally looking at him. "Maybe they're trying hard and just not getting it still? I mean, I was trying really hard in my skills class Friday and still ended up with this stupid bruise. It's starting to look pretty nasty."

I pulled up the sleeve of my shirt to show off the discolored welt. Peter reached out and rubbed his fingers over the bruise on my right arm, feeling the bump under the skin that was now a much deeper purple and blue than the day before when he had last seen it. His fingers running over my skin gave me a cold chill, goose bumps popping up on my arm instantly.

"Sorry," he smiled, pulling his hand back quickly.

"I don't know if I will still try out next year," I began again. "But for right now I think the new team might help me see my potential a little more. And might help me get a chance to really push my skills. It's not going to be easy, but I think that's the real reason I don't like Blast anymore. I like the girls and the gym and everything, but it's just so easy that it feels like a waste of my time more often than not."

"What's your favorite thing about the gym?" Peter asked me, his question catching me off guard.

"I guess my skills class," I said after thinking it over for a minute. "I get to learn new things with people who really want to get better."

"Do the girls on your team want to get better at the things they're not hitting?"

"Yeah, I think so," I shrugged. "Lexi does really well and hits everything, but I know she has private flying lessons a few times a month. And I guess the other girls on the team are still kind of younger, so maybe they want to do better but they just can't control their body a whole lot."

"Cheerleading is confusing," Peter said with a little bit of a sigh. "But maybe you're just too good for your own good. You know?"

"No," I laughed. "I don't know what you're saying at all."

"It's all really easy for you," he explained. "It's just one more thing you're really good at. I don't think there is a single sport in the world that you're not amazing at. But not everyone is like you. Maybe some of the girls are trying as hard as you, but they just can't do what you're doing yet."

I thought about his words for a minute, and I realized it was true. I looked at him for a long minute, just sitting there on my bed petting Storm, who was fast asleep on his lap. The fact that he was able to figure out my struggle at the gym so easily and lay it all out in a way that made perfect sense was a little shocking. But, it was exactly what he had done.

"When did you get so smart?" I asked him, frustrated that I didn't think about things like that in the first place.

"I blame you," he joked. "Now that you're a cheerleader you're basically a ditzy airhead so I have to do all the thinking to make up for you."

Although I knew he was kidding, I slowly picked up Thunder and set him on my pillows, then I reached over and took Storm from Peter and did the same. As I set the second sleeping kitten down, it clicked for Peter what I was about to do. Knowing I was clearly going to hit him, Peter sprang up off my bed and raced out of my room. With a laugh I got up and followed him, glad for a chance to not only get back at him but also put the thoughts of cheerleading out of my mind for a little while.

CHAPTER 13

"That bruise is getting worse," Lexi commented as we sat drinking water after Tuesday night's Blast practice. Sadly, my bruise was just one of the things getting worse. The practice was full of bobbled stunts despite the changes Halley and Lexi assured me went great when I wasn't there Thursday night. Sure, everyone was more or less staying in the air, but they all looked wobbly aside from Lexi and myself.

"I bumped it Sunday wrestling Peter," I admitted with a laugh. "But it's okay. I won."

"You were actually wrestling him?" Lexi asked with the raise of her eyebrow.

"Yeah, he called me an airhead cheerleader so I had to put him in his place," I said like it was the simplest thing in the world. Lexi, as always when I talked about my interactions with Peter, looked beyond confused.

"Well, are you ready for practice?" Lexi asked, pointing to where some of the girls on Fuze were warming up at the far end of the gym.

"I hope so," I said with a frown. "I'm already a little tired from all those full outs and now I have to go learn a whole new routine."

"You're going to do great," she assured me. "If you want I can stay and cheer you on the whole time."

"Thanks, but I don't know how Nicole would feel about that." I stood up and walked towards my bag then, knowing it would be a good idea to head over to my new team. "I'll text you as soon as I leave tonight."

"Deal," she said with a sigh before giving me a hug and heading to where Matthew was waiting to drive her home. He gave me a wave that I quickly returned before walking across the gym to where Nicole and the girls in purple were getting ready.

"Are you excited, Max?" Nicole asked me as I stuffed my bag in a cubby closer to the mat we would be on for my practice with Fuze. She had also just come from Blast's practice, although it was a lot less physically demanding for her.

"A little," I said with my best attempt at a smile. I was feeling about as nervous as the first time I practiced with Blast. I only hoped I didn't have to stand up and awkwardly talk about my family again.

"You're going to do great," she said to me, mirroring Lexi's words exactly. "Let me introduce you to your stunt group."

Following Nicole, I was taken over to meet three girls that were clearly excited to see me. I recognized them from seeing them around competitions and at the gym, but I didn't know any of them by name until Nicole introduced them to me. Juleah was my back spot, and she was hard to miss with her long wavy red hair. Even up in a ponytail, it reached almost to her waist. Her hair was the reddest hair I had ever seen and looked amazing next to her pale skin and bright blue eyes. My side bases were Payten and Erin, both of whom were practically a foot taller than me. Or at least a good 8 inches. Payten had black micro-braided hair that featured tiny purple beads at the end of each strand that perfectly matched her Fuze tank top and shorts. She had dark skin and huge eyes that made her look more like a model standing on the mat then a cheerleader. Erin had hair about the same length as mine, but it had chunky blond highlights that went well with her thick eyeliner and dark hazel eyes. Her skin was super tan, and unlike some girls I saw at the gym, it didn't look sprayed on or from a tanning bed.

After only a minute to learn their names and say hello, it was time to get started. We did some basic conditioning and warm-ups, including having my stunt team getting me in the air to try some basic baskets so they could get used to flying me. Only having three people holding me in the air was a little strange so soon after Blast practice. But the skills I was doing in the air were pretty much things I learned my first week at cheer, so that made it a little better. Once we were all warmed up I sat at the side and watched as the girls ran the routine with all the flying stunts, but only marking everything else. That meant the fliers were always in the air at the usual times, but all of the tumbling and even the dance was just walked through. It helped me see the more difficult portion of the routine from the other girls, and also get a feel for the flying I would be doing. Payten, Erin, and Juleah held their arms as if they were holding me up for each stunt, and based on the other fliers performing the skills I was able to pretty much see where I would be and what I would be doing.

"Let's run it again with the dance included, but this time, I want Max and her stunt team to go over to mat 3 and start learning everything," Nicole called out.

I followed her instructions and was happy to see Tonya waiting on the mat to work with us. She gave me a big smile as I joined her, squeezing me surprisingly tight for someone as tiny as I was.

"I'm so proud of you Max," Tonya said once she finally let me go. "You filling in for Cassidy is going to be perfect."

"Now I just have to learn everything," I said with a nervous laugh.

"If anyone can do it, you can," she assured me then launched into teaching me the various stunts and skills of the Fuze routine.

My fears and worries were gone instantly as I realized that working with the new stunt team was a lot like working with my stunt group on Blast. Not only did Juleah always give me encouragement right before I went into the air like Halley did, I was apparently a lot lighter than Cassidy so once they figured out the grips for my foot size, everything was smooth sailing.

"That was perfect," Juleah told me with a massive smile after I was tossed up to do a kick single. Having girls that were a little taller and stronger than my stunt team on Blast made the move a lot easier to get enough height for the skill. In fact, if it was allowed on a level 4 team, I think I could have added a second rotation based on how high I was thrown.

"Let's try that whole section in a row," Tonya suggested after we had done all of the skills on their own. "We can slow it down if we need to, but I want to see it all laid out."

"Including the basket?" I asked, going through the steps in my mind.

"If you're okay with that," she said with a smile. When I nodded we started at the beginning and started the second try.

As Erin, Payton, and Juleah lifted me up, I spun around once before standing in a liberty pose with my left leg bent while my right leg was being held up by the girls below me. Then, as the girls dipped me down and back up, I traded feet so I was standing on my left foot. Once I was standing for a few counts as I moved my arms in the choreography Tonya had taught me, I lifted my left leg up next to my head to hold it in place. I held the heel stretch while doing some additional sweeping arm motions as well as a few specific facial expressions. From there I twisted my body around so I was facing my right and made my arms into a 'T' while my left leg was straight out in the air behind me. As I held the arabesque, Tonya counted while the girls below me lowered their arms just to raise them right back up while I grabbed my left foot behind my head with both hands. The now familiar scorpion was easy to hold until I moved to hold my left leg out with my hand gripping my calf in a move called a scale. I even managed an over the top smile before returning to the arabesque then brought my legs together. Once the girls under me moved so I was once again facing where the crowd would be, I folded my body over and flipped forward while hugging my legs in a move known as a fortune cookie. As my feet hit the mat one at a time, I stood up with a smile before jumping back into their arms for the final basket toss which consisted of a basic toe touch. All in all, it only took a few eight counts to complete, but when it was done we all celebrated like it had been a full routine.

"How did you get those transitions that fast?" Payten asked, staring at me in shock once the sequence was over.

"I don't know," I shrugged. "They just kind of happened."

"I'm not happy Cassidy got hurt," Juleah began slowly. "But if it means you're filling her spot then I'm kind of okay with it."

"Just don't tell Cassidy that," Erin warned her, although she had a smile on her face.

The rest of the evening was spent running the skills with my new stunt team while Tonya helped to make sure I was getting everything down properly. And for the most part, I really was. Between my extra skills class and my time on Blast, I was able to pick up everything pretty quickly. I knew learning the flying skills was just the first part of the equation, but it seemed to be the part everyone else was most concerned with. The dance was intimidating me a little, but before I left for the evening Tonya pulled me aside to set up a time to go over it with her.

"Can you get here a little early on Thursday?" She asked me, pulling out her phone to check her schedule. "I'll be here helping Nitro clean up some changes, so I can walk you through everything a few times."

"Yeah, I can stay," I answered, knowing my schedule was wide open between the end of school and the start of my practice time for Blast.

"Try watching the routine a few times between now and then as well," Tonya added, pulling up her YouTube app. "The most recent version of the routine was posted about a week ago on the gym's channel. Here it is."

I watched over her shoulder for a few seconds, taking note of some of the motions I had seen performed live earlier. She stopped it part of the way in, then copied the link and texted it to my phone. I could hear my phone buzz from the pocket of my cheer bag almost instantly.

"Do you know what tumbling passes I'll be doing?" I asked her, knowing it would be something I could work on before the next practice.

"Nope," she said quickly. "But Nicole can write it all down for you I'm sure. I'm sure none of it will be all that hard for you to pick up."

"Fingers crossed," I managed before yawning.

"You did great tonight Max, now go home and get some sleep."

With a quick thank you, I turned and walked to my cubby to get my cheer bag. Pulling my phone out, I saw a series of missed messages from Lexi. I knew she was going to want full details about practice, but first I had to actually make it home without falling asleep. All the flying and tumbling of two teams' worth of practices was catching up to me quickly.

"Awesome job tonight Max," Nicole said to me then. She was walking my way holding a glittery purple gym bag. "You don't need to use the bag if you don't want to, but there are a few practice uniforms in there, your Fuze bow, and your new uniform. Let me know if you need anything else that we might have forgotten."

"Thanks, Nicole," I said with a smile, which was followed by yet another a yawn.

"Now get out of here before you fall asleep on the mat," Nicole laughed.

Knowing she wasn't too far from the truth, I turned and headed for the door. On the way out I said goodbye to a few of the girls from Fuze that were still in the gym, then made a beeline for my dad's car. I shoved the purple glitter bag into the back seat then flopped down into the upholstery as I typed a text to Lexi.

"Bad practice?" my dad asked, giving me a concerned look.

"It was great," I said quickly, realizing how my entrance might have confused him. "I'm just totally ready for bed after all that."

"Your wish is my command," he said with a wave of his hand as he started the car and took off towards home. I knew it would be a miracle if I was awake for the whole drive, even if it was only a few short miles.

CHAPTER 14

As much as I loved flying, tumbling was by far my favorite thing about cheerleading. It was something I did on my own without anyone helping or holding me up, and was something I was excelling at but still had room to learn new skills. Sure, on Blast I was limited to round offs, back handsprings, and back tucks. But, now that I was also on Fuze, I was getting harder tumbling passes to work on and bring to the mat.

"Let's try that again but make sure you really push off strong going into that last back handspring before your layout," Greg suggested as he worked with me on tumbling.

Rather than try the passes alone at home in the backyard, I decided to come in and work on one of the open gym mats by myself for the evening. I was doing okay on my own, but Greg, of course, had to step in and see how much farther he could push me to get even more out of my tumbling.

Standing at the corner of the mat I ran and jumped hard before throwing my body into a simple round off. From there I did a back handspring then a whip before a back handspring and a final layout. The whip and layout were the same general motion as a back tuck, only I kept my legs straight. This made the move a little harder and also worth more on the raw score while performing. After all the flips and twists and turns I landed on the ground and took a few steps back thanks to the momentum, but stayed on the blue mat and also on my feet. It was a lot harder of a tumbling pass than anything I did with Blast, and if felt good to do it knowing I would be able to perform it at a competition and in front of a whole crowd of people.

"How was that?" I asked Greg, who was frozen in place.

"Are you kidding me right now?" he asked in reply, a smile growing on his face.

"That was perfect Max. And your height on the whip at the end was amazing."

"Thanks," I grinned, glad to know I was doing well enough to impress Greg to that level. Thanks to my time in my skills classes he got to see me fall a lot as I tried new skills like kick fulls and even standing double fulls, but now I was able to show him the power I could put behind intermediate tumbling. I was itching for the day I could throw a full on the mats, but knew it would likely be a few years until I was on a level 5 squad and was finally allowed to, according to the score sheets. Which of course was only a maybe, considering I hadn't made a decision about my cheerleading career after Summit just yet.

"So that's your elite tumbling pass right before pyramid," Greg said as he pulled out a half sheet of paper from his pocket that Nicole had given him. It listed all the tumbling passes I would do in the routine with Fuze. "You have a roundoff back handspring back tuck sequence with three other girls, but you will need to work with them on getting the timing just right. And then the other major one is the back handspring layout near the start of the routine. The standing jumps are almost identical as Blast, just with an extra toe touch before the back tuck."

"That's really it?" I asked as I took my cheer bow out so I could fix my ponytail that had gotten loose thanks to the tumbling. I was wearing my new purple Fuze practice wear complete with the purple ombre bow, but since the bow was new I was struggling to get the ponytail holder to stretch how I wanted it to. With a sigh as I wrestled with the frustrating hair situation, I muttered, "I'm about ready to cut all of my hair off."

"Are you okay?" Greg asked, laughing as I finally got my hair and the bow to cooperate.

"My hair is just driving me crazy," I explained. "I usually don't have it this long, but I have to if I want it to look normal with my bow and everything."

"Or just cut it and wear it half up for cheer," he commented.

His words made me freeze instantly. I stared at Greg, trying to figure out why I hadn't thought of that on my own. When I first started at the gym Lexi had hair just barely long enough for a ponytail, so at practices she often wore it only half up. She was growing it for competition season, so I always assumed it was more or less a rule for all of us to have hair long enough for a high ponytail. The more I thought about it though, the more I realized there were a lot of girls at competitions that had shorter hair they still could put in a poof and half ponytail complete with bow and everything. Most of the time they would skip curling their hair, but even if they did add curls, it was sure to be a lot less work than trying to use a wand on a whole head of long hair. Although there weren't any girls at the TNT Force gym that I could call to mind with shorter hair, it apparently wasn't against the rules. Or at least I assumed as much after Greg suggested the haircut.

"This is why you're my favorite Greg," I said as the enormity of it set in. "I wonder if my barber will know how to cut it cute and short and everything."

"Hold on," Greg said, holding up a hand to stop me. "Your barber? As in a barber shop?"

"Yeah," I nodded. "I go with my dad when he gets his hair done. The guy does fine."

"I'm going to pretend I didn't just hear that," Greg said with the shake of his head. "I have five sisters, and if they heard that they would die of shock. I'll be right back."

As Greg walked away I shrugged off his rather dramatic response and went back to trying the tumbling pass. I already had it down, but it was still good to run it a few more times. After the third time I landed it, Greg still hadn't returned. So, I simply walked over and began packing up my gym bag, finally ready to end my practice time. I slipped a pair of gray basketball shorts over my uniform automatically. I didn't always wear them while biking home lately, but after the reaction Cate had to the news of me being on cheerleading squad, I felt a little more self-conscious. Walking towards the office to find Greg, I paused to watch Nitro finish a full out. I thought it might be nice to say hi to Connor before I left the gym, but sadly he wasn't the only person who noticed I was watching practice.

"So it's true," Leanne said, pointing at my purple bow. "You're filling Cassidy's spot."

"Yup," I said with a polite smile. Connor was talking to TJ so I didn't feel like I could walk away to go talk to him to get away from Leanne like I wanted to.

"They were totally going to give the spot to me, but it's not really fair to have a level Summit5 athlete fill a spot on a level 4 team," she said with a dramatic flip of her curly blonde hair. "It would be like sending in a professional to do the job of an amateur. So you're a much better fit. As long as you can actually land the skills."

I opened my mouth to respond but was distracted when Greg called my name. Without so much as a goodbye to Leanne, I turned and walked towards the office where Greg was waiting with Tonya.

"You really get your hair cut by a barber?" Tonya asked, a shocked look on her face.

"Ummm yeah," I said, suddenly feeling embarrassed by the fact.

"Okay, what are you doing Saturday morning?" she asked, a seriously stressed look on her face.

"Nothing, I think," I shrugged, confused by her question.

"Good, I'm making you a hair appointment." Tonya pulled out her phone and began flipping through her contacts. "My cousin is a hairdresser and has a studio in town. I'll see when she can fit you in and text you tonight."

"Can't I just call her?" I asked, feeling like me getting my hair done shouldn't be such a production.

"Probably," Tonya nodded. "But this is a big deal. Your first proper haircut. You need someone there with you to help celebrate. We can even go get our nails painted after. Trust me, girls need this kind of thing sometimes."

I stared at her, feeling a little overwhelmed. But, part of me was happy to have her help. After all, I was just getting to the age of fun days around town with mom when she started getting sick. And as much as I loved my dad, there were some girl things he didn't understand. The first time I told him I needed to go buy a sports bra for cheerleading he had to call Peter and Kyle's mom for backup. Now, thankfully, he just gives me money and a ride to the mall if I need anything of that nature.

"Thanks, Tonya," I finally said. I still wasn't totally convinced my barber couldn't manage to cut my hair shorter, but it was nice to know I was going to get a fancy haircut like the other girls at the gym.

"You're welcome," Tonya replied with a big smile. "We can't let you hit the mat looking anything less than your best at Summit. Especially since you're going to be up there twice representing TNT."

The reminder of everything the next two weeks would hold popped back into my mind and I instantly had the urge to go back and practice my tumbling a little more. I fought the feeling, knowing that I was going to need to save energy for Blast's practice Thursday night. Saying thanks to Greg and Tonya once more I headed for the door. As I slipped on my bike helmet and clipped the chin strap, I was a bit surprised when I looked up and saw Connor exiting the gym and coming my way.

"Finally, I caught you," he grinned, walking over and wrapping me in a big and sweaty hug.

"What was that for?" I asked with a smile on my face as he finally let me go.

"Just a little congrats on making it onto Fuze," he explained. "Texting isn't the same as a hug."

"True," I agreed. "I don't get your sweat all over me in a text."

"Sorry about that," he laughed.

"It's okay, I'm sweaty from tumbling too," I assured him.

"Connor, let's go," Leanne called out then, shooting me a glare from where she stood at the open gym door.

"On my way," he said to her before turning back to give me one final hug. "I'll see you tomorrow."

"See ya," I said giving him a wave before climbing onto my bike.

Despite Leanne's judging looks and even her annoying comments about me joining Fuze, nothing could dampen my mood. I was doing some awesome new tumbling passes, I was going to get to skip curling my hair after getting it cut with Tonya, and Connor went out of his way to congratulate me. As simple as it was for Connor to make sure to talk to me before I left the gym, it still made me feel really special for some reason. It helped the ride home fly by, even after spending the evening working out with Greg.

CHAPTER 15

"Like, how short is short?" Halley asked me as we sat putting on our shoes at the start of Blast practice on Thursday night. I had already been at the gym for over an hour working on choreography for the Fuze routine, but that practice time was just with Tonya. When I delivered the news to my friends once they arrived, they were instantly freaking out about it way more than I thought they would.

"I don't know," I said honestly. "Just shorter than how it is now. That way I can just put half of it up for competitions and all that."

"Are you getting like layers or highlights or like an angle or anything?" Lexi asked, her face lit up at the idea of my hair makeover.

"No idea."

"Tonya isn't telling you anything?" Halley tried again.

"I didn't really ask her," I admitted. "She just said we were going Saturday morning at 10:30. That's all I know."

"I would be freaking out if I was you," Anna chimed in. "This is seriously major."

I was planning to again explain to the girls that it wasn't a big deal or anything but was saved when Nicole announced it was time to get started. Moving to stand on my familiar spot, we began with our usual exercises and warmups before launching into the routine that was becoming more natural to everyone. Although I had only been at one practice since the last round of changes, I was easily landing all the skills, tumbling, and even additional dance elements that had been added. I was also happy to see that a few of the girls were staying in the air through most of our full outs. It made me worried that they weren't super consistent, but I could only hope and pray they would get better on it over the next week and a half.

"We leave in 12 days ladies," Nicole reminded us as we were taking a break between full outs. It was like she was reading my mind. "If you only hit three times, let those times be on that stage at Summit. You don't want to walk away with another second place."

"Wow, that was harsh," I mumbled, taking a long sip of my water.

"What do you mean?" Halley asked me as she re-tied her cheer shoes.

"She just rubbed in us not winning this season," I reminded her.

"That's not what she was talking about," Halley said instantly. "She's talking about last year at Summit. And the year before. This will be Blast's third year at summit, and every year so far we've ended up in second place. It's like we can do just enough to make it to the finals and then do kind of great, but for one reason or another, we don't quite go far enough. We've always bobbled something and dropped just enough points that we can't win."

"You mean in three years the team never hit in the finals?" I asked, wanting to make sure I understood.

"Not just in the finals," she explained. "We've never hit at Summit at all. I think that's why Nicole isn't pushing us too hard right now. If we can just hit what we have and be confident about it then we can maybe finally land a clean routine. If we can hit at least once we might maybe, possibly, kind of have a chance at winning."

I let Halley's words sink in as we continued to run the routine. Watching the girls around me, I saw that the reason they weren't hitting the new routine had more to do with timing issues and not being used to the changes in positioning than not actually being able to hold the moves in the air. It was like people were getting used to everything that had changed, and as things got more comfortable they were getting better. Once we had hit the routine twice in a row, Nicole announced that we were going to call it a night.

"Wait," I said out loud, speaking before I could stop myself. Everyone stopped and looked at me. Clearly, like me, they were not sure why I had spoken up. "I have an idea."

There were thirty pairs of eyes on me, Nicole standing with her arms crossed over her chest. At first, I thought she was annoyed, but I quickly saw she looked very intrigued. In fact, as I began letting the girls know my idea, a smile blossomed on her face.

"We just hit twice, but I feel like we're finally getting into the groove of things," I said, praying I wouldn't lose my confidence before I got out all that I wanted to say. "Now that we're finally getting used to the routine and we're all getting it where it needs to be, why don't we keep going?"

"But practice is over," someone called out. I was too nervous about being the center of attention to figure out who had spoken.

"Yeah, but every time we come back to the gym it's like we forget that we can do it," I replied, remembering that we hit the routine towards the end of the night at Tuesday's practice as well. "So why not use the momentum we have right now and see how far we can go? I think we should run the routine until we drop a stunt. It might just be one more time, but what if we can say we have to do it four or five times before we mess up? I know I'd feel a lot better going into Summit if I knew we were able to hit a whole lot all in a row."

"What if we can't make it through anymore right now?" Anna asked although I could already see a determined look on her face.

"Then we're done," Lexi said, taking over before I could speak up. "And at next practice, we see if we can beat just twice in a row."

"I'm in," Halley announced, looking around to see who else was going to agree.

I didn't realize it at first, but I was more or less holding my breath. After speaking up with the idea to really push ourselves, I was suddenly nervous that only my best friends would think the idea was a good one. But, as one girl and then another followed by another also announced that they were ready to try, I could feel the energy on the mat changing. It was like everyone was on board with the idea, and not just to try it one more time. It was clear that people were ready to run the routine as many times as it took, to prove we could do it.

"Alright ladies," Nicole called out, the biggest smile on her face that I had ever seen aside from maybe the day we won our bid to Summit. "Let's get in place for the start of the routine."

As the music familiar to Blast filled the gym, the energy that started building moments before suddenly seemed to triple. When we normally ran the routine full out, people would perform a lot, but not quite the same as when we were in front of an audience. But this time, it was different. This time, everyone was performing like we were on that final stage at Summit, going for the grand prize. The energy was electric, and as we reached our final poses without a single mistake people were actually excited to set up and run it again. And again. And again.

Running everything full out for the seventh time of the night without a mistake was starting to get everyone's attention. Nitro actually stopped their practice and came to watch and cheer us on. Even the athletes that were at the gym to practice skills on an open mat came over to watch. We had gotten a lot farther that I thought without a fall, and despite having a regular length practice before starting the extra full outs, all of the girls on Blast were still giving it everything they had.

"From the top!" Nicole called out, causing an explosion of cheers.

We set back up and made it halfway through the routine for the eighth time when, based on the gathering crowd's reaction, I knew we must have finally dropped a stunt. We finished the routine though, and as we reached the end of the performance there was just as much cheering as when we had hit everything perfectly.

"Seven!" Nicole called out as we were finally quieting down and ending the hugs and high-fives. "You did awesome ladies."

"Next time we're going for eight!" Lexi announced, causing all the girls on the mat to cheer even more.

"Now get out of here and get some rest!" Nicole said in response. She was smiling though, clearly proud of all we had done.

"That was such a good idea," Halley said to me as we were finally getting a much needed drink of water. "If we can keep that kind of attitude until Summits over then we might finally win."

"Fingers crossed, right?" I shrugged, although I was still grinning.

"No crossing fingers needed, that was amazing!" Turning, I saw that it was Connor who had spoken. "I don't think Nitro has even gone that many times full out without a mistake."

"Not yet at least," I told him, finishing off my water and slipping the empty bottle into my bag. "You still have a few days until Worlds."

"If only we had you on our squad to get us pumped up like that," he said as he reached over and picked up my bag for me.

Connor walked me to the door then, chatting with me about Nitro's upcoming trip to Worlds. It was nice to not only have my bag carried for me after working out for so long, but also to just hang out with Connor for a bit. We usually had time to hang out some while we were both practicing at the gym, not to mention the time we spent texting. But with the extra practices that came with joining a second squad, my time spent at the gym was always busy.

"Wait," I finally said when we made it to where my dad was waiting near the office. "I won't see you again before you leave for Worlds, will I?"

"I don't think so," he replied after thinking it over. "We leave super early Monday, and I won't be in the gym until we get back."

"In that case, good luck!" I reached up and gave Connor a hug, something I would never have done even a few months before. "Text me as soon as you get off the mat every time."

"I will," he assured me before finally ending the long embrace. "And hopefully, I'll see you once you guys get to Orlando."

"Hopefully," I agreed, then turned to leave the gym.

CHAPTER 16

The news about our seven perfect full outs got around the gym fast. I was just thankful that we didn't try to match or better the record at Fuze practice Friday night. Instead, we worked on running the routine in sections so everyone could clean it up, and also so I could finish learning everything. It was a little hard to remember all of the skills and motions, but I was more or less able to get in the right place at the right time. When I finally did my flying skills towards the end of practice, I thankfully stayed in the air every time with only a few bobbles, which were largely due to me trying to remember the order of everything.

"Your timing is coming along nicely," Tonya said to me as I was packing up at the end other night. She didn't help me with the flying as much as the previous practice, but was still there to watch a lot of our time on the mat. "Are you excited for tomorrow?"

"Tomorrow?" I asked her, my brain suddenly trying to remember if I said I was going to be at the gym for something.

"Your hair?"

"Oh yeah!" I said with a laugh. "Sorry, I've been so busy working on the routine and worrying about Summit that I haven't really been thinking about it."

"That's okay," she smiled. "As long as you're ready to go in the morning then it's all good."

"I'll be ready, I promise," I assured her.

"And wear flip flops," Tonya added.

"Flip flops?" I asked, slipping on my backpack to leave.

"I told you we're going to the nail salon too, right?" She paused at my look of confusion. "I might have just told your dad. But yes, you need flip flops so you can get your nails painted. And then we can do lunch before I drop you off at home." When I stared at her in

164

shock for a minute Tonya went on. "I always do a spa day the weekend before Worlds with my best friend Janet, but she's at a wedding in Dallas until Tuesday. So, you get to fill her spot."

"I don't think I've painted my nails in the last five years," I said honestly, trying to wrap my head around the girly day Tonya clearly had planned.

"I promise I won't make you pick neon colors or anything too crazy," she assured me. "But trust me when I say that everyone needs a girl's day once in a while to just get pampered."

"Lexi and Halley would agree with you I think," I said, remembering their constant attempts to do my makeup or put me in girly dresses when we had slumber parties. "As long as I get to pick where we go for lunch, then I'm okay with all of it."

Or at least that was what I thought until I was picked up in the morning. Tonya was wearing a fancy and frilly white and pink strapless dress and wedge sandals that made her look at least 5 inches taller. It made me feel out of place in my jean shorts and blue V-neck short sleeve shirt. I tried to remind myself that it was all going to be worth it if I got shorter hair and didn't need to spend as much time styling it before competitions.

The atmosphere walking into the Style Shack after the short drive from my home was a lot to take in. As soon as we entered the salon I could smell the hair products in the air. Getting past that, I took in the room around me. It was a fairly small space, all decorated in silver and black. The walls were actually painted black but were decorated with black and white photos of girls with their hair done in fancy styles and cuts to keep it from being too dark and overwhelming. There were only six stations for cutting hair and a small hair washing station near the back. A door led to the bathrooms and back storage room, which was located next to fancy chairs like ones I had seen in movies with large domes that women would sit under to dry their hair.

"You must be Max," a tall woman grinned while stepping towards me. Aside from her bright red lipstick, she was wearing all black. Literally, even her hair and eye makeup was black. It might have been a lot on other people, but it was all done in a way that actually looked nice. Her makeup was thick but not too much, and her hair had lots of layers and was curled to keep it from looking too edgy. Her smile also helped me warm up to her as I shook her hand.

"Yeah," I replied in answer to her question.

"It's so good to meet you, Max. I'm Laura."

As she spoke she motioned me to the back of the salon. Tonya thankfully followed us. We started the appointment with a hair wash that was basically the best thing I had ever experienced. Aside from maybe the massage chairs you can pay a dollar to sit on in the mall, it was one of the most relaxing few minutes of my life. It was something they never did at the barber shop, so I was beginning to warm up to Tonya and her plan for me quickly. When we made it to Laura's hair cutting station, she finally asked the question I was also dying to hear the answer to.

"So what are we doing with your hair today?" Laura asked as she covered me with a black cape and snapped it closed around my neck.

"We want a cute inverted bob with a little bit of facial framing and longer layers so it lays simply but can still be styled up as needed," Tonya explained easily

"What?" I asked in response to all that Tonya had just said to Laura.

"It was just a fancy way of saying you want it kind of like my haircut, but with a little less length since you don't want a wave like I do," Tonya explained like it was all extremely simple.

"Don't worry sweetie, I'll take good care of you," Laura said as she began twisting my hair and holding it up in place with large claw clips. "So this is your first time at a real hair salon?"

"Yup," I nodded, only to have Laura hold my head in place. "My mom used to cut my hair when I was little, and after she was gone my dad just started taking me to the barber shop where he gets his hair done."

"Did your parents get divorced?" Laura asked, giving me a confused look through the mirror on the wall in front of me.

"No, she died of cancer," I said simply, knowing it was likely going to cause a big reaction from Laura.

"Oh my goodness!" she gasped. "I'm so sorry to hear that Max."

"Thanks," I said with a polite smile. Laura's response was similar to most other people's reaction, so I had a standard answer ready to go. "My dad is a research scientist and is determined to cure cancer so no one else has to suffer like she did. That will make it all mean more."

"I hope he does," Laura said with a nod. "I have an aunt that had breast cancer that she almost didn't beat. That was hard enough to go through, so I can only image what it would be like to lose a parent that way." Laura paused. "So how long have you been cheering at TNT?"

I knew Laura was trying to change the subject, and I was okay with it. Talking about my mom didn't bother me too much since it was something that I was reminded of a dozen times every day. It wasn't as hard as it was a couple of years ago but was still not something I would consider easy. So, the chance to talk about cheerleading, the gym, being on two teams and Summit was a great distraction. In fact, it was a big enough distraction that when Laura announced that she was all done with my hair I thought it was a joke.

"Ready for the big reveal?" Laura asked after removing the cape that was covering me and brushing off any hair that made it onto my shirt.

I knew she had been chopping, snipping, blow drying and straightening my hair, but at that moment I had no idea what I would see when I was turned around. At

Tonya's insistence, I hadn't been facing the mirror since the haircut began. I was a little nervous, but the look on Tonya's face when I was halfway around in the spin told me that my new do must have been good.

"What?" I said to my reflection, not quite recognizing myself.

My hair was still its same light brown color and I was still wearing the same clothing. But other than that I looked like a totally different person. My hair was now cut short, stopping just below my chin. It was cut on an angle so the hair at the back of my head was shorter than it was near my face. Speaking of my face, it looked somehow older and more mature with the haircut. I stared at the mirror in shock at how much a few inches of hair could change how I looked. And then I turned my head and watched as my hair swished and moved. I didn't think I cared that much about my hair, but watching it in that moment I couldn't help an even larger grin growing on my face.

"It's adorable!" Tonya finally gushed, all but jumping up and down. "This is the perfect cut for you Max."

"I didn't know it could look like this," I said simply, reaching up to run my fingers through my hair.

"And it will look even cuter half up," Laura explained, holding the front section of my hair up so I could see how it would kind of look for Summit. "You can do the poof like usual and then tease just a little bit here before you pop your bow right there."

I watched her instructions and honestly was excited to go home and give it a try. But, I knew there was still a lot more of the day to come. As we walked towards the door after I paid using the money my dad had given me, I gave Laura a hug and thanked her for my new haircut. I also took one of her business cards and assured her I would never go to the barber shop for a cut again. She made me promise as kind of as a joke, but after seeing how great my hair looked, I knew it was the best choice. Besides, spending the time chatting about cheerleading while getting my hair done was honestly a lot less girly and lame than I assumed it would be.

CHAPTER 17

Three hours later, Tonya dropped me off at home wearing a new outfit, carrying shopping bags, and looking like a whole new person. Tonya hinted something about my dad mentioning my clothing or something, then all but insisted we head to the mall. I figured there was more to the story, but she wasn't exactly ready to tell me just then. So, after our nail salon appointment was done and I was already so far off the deep end, I just went with it. I mean, I really should have expected it considering the wad of cash my dad gave me when I left the house.

At the nail salon, Tonya got her finger and toenails painted a super bright pink complete with a sparkly top coat. I thought it was a bit much, but then I remembered that she was the head coach for Bomb Squad, so she was choosing to match her team's hot pink uniform and bows. When I realized that, I decided that matching my team would be a good idea too. So, I went with a bright red nail polish on my fingers for Blast, and bright purple on my toes for Fuze. No one would really see my toes, but I figured it was the thought that counted for that one. We both got a gel nail polish that Tonya told me would stay on through all of Summit. I knew I wouldn't be coating my fingers in color again anytime soon, so it was nice to know it would last a while so people could take it in before it was gone for good.

When we got to the mall I tried to make it clear that I was a t-shirt and shorts kind of girl. But, Tonya wanted me to try at least one thing I normally wouldn't. And that was a dress. We went to a few stores that were way too flashy but then ended up at Target where she picked out a nice red and white dress that was really simple while still being cute. Announcing that my black flip flops wouldn't go with the dress Tonya also picked out a pair of gold strappy sandals for me. I was only going to try them on and then leave before buying anything, but then Tonya explained that TNT always had an end of the season banquet and everyone was asked to dress up. It was the real reason we had even gone shopping. While we were still in the store she admitted to me that my dad heard about the banquet and knew I had nothing to wear. So, with a sigh, I bought the dress. I was determined to only wear it at the banquet, but in the end, Tonya insisted I wore it out of the store so we would look extra fancy at lunch.

By the time I made it home, after a large BBQ lunch at what turned out to be Tonya's favorite spot in town as well as my own, I was feeling exhausted and ready to change. I knew my dad would want to see my hair and dress before I put on normal clothing, though. After calling his name in the house a few times without a reply I was confused as to where he was. I knew he wasn't at work, and yet he wasn't at home like I expected him to be. So, when I saw Peter and Kyle playing in the pool through the back patio door I walked out immediately. In that moment I was so focused on finding my dad I didn't even think about what I was wearing.

"Hey!" I called out, getting their attention instantly. "Do you know where my dad is?"

"Yeah, he's- what are you wearing?"

Kyle's question caught me so off guard I froze completely for a few seconds. I just stood there and stared at the boys swimming in the pool and tried to think of what to say. Finally, I managed, "Tonya took me shopping after I got my hair cut."

"You look like a girl," Kyle said again, a rather confused look on his face.

"I am a girl," I reminded him simply.

"But you look like one," he added. "You even painted your nails. You never do that."

"Well," I said trying to think of an answer quickly. "My coach wanted to take me for a girl's day after we got my hair done. I only got my nails painted so they'll look good for Summit."

"So why are you wearing a dress?" At Kyle's question, I looked at Peter who was standing waist deep in the water just watching me. I couldn't tell what he was thinking one way or another thanks to the strange look on his face

"Why does it matter?" I replied, starting to get a little annoyed at how Kyle was reacting. "You've seen me in my cheerleading uniform a bunch of times, and that's a skirt."

"This's different," Kyle said quickly. "You wear that when you do cool stuff and flip around and all that. That's not something thing a lot of girls can do."

"I can still do stunts even if I'm wearing a dress," I told him, although in that moment I knew I wasn't going to even try if he asked me to. Without cheer shorts on under my dress, it would not be a good idea.

"It's still weird," Kyle said one last time then turned and started swimming around the shallow end of the pool once again.

Glancing at Peter, I saw that he was still just staring at me, with the same unreadable expression on his face. With a sigh, I turned and walked back into the house. Kyle was annoying me for sure, but more than that, I actually wanted to swim. Walking down the hallways to my room, I tossed the shopping bags that had the outfit I wore out of the house near my closet and started looking for my swimsuit in my dresser. Digging out my dark green one piece, I tossed it onto my bed and started to unbuckle my new sandals. While I attempted to remove the shoe I heard someone walking down the hallway towards my room.

"What?" I said in a less than kind voice when Peter appeared in my bedroom doorway.

"Uh, hi," he said with an exaggerated shrug. He only looked at me for a second then shifted his eyes to stare down at the floor.

"Did you come in here to tell me I look like a girl too?" I asked, finally getting one of my sandals off after struggling with it for what felt like forever.

"No," Peter assured me, his eyes still locked on the carpet.

"Well, then what do you want?" I was losing my patience with both Peter and the other sandal that was still strapped onto my foot.

"You, um," he began, before clearing his throat and trying again. "You look really nice."

"What?" I asked, stopping in my attempt to remove my sandal and looked at him.

He looked pretty ridiculous. He stood there, his wet swim trunks dripping water onto the carpet, and his curly black hair matted to his head and dripping water onto his bare shoulders.

"I just wanted to let you know that you look really nice," he finally said, his eyes moving from the carpet to actually look at me. "Kyle was just being weird. But your hair and nails and the dress and everything is really nice. It's just, well, nice."

"You said that already," I reminded him.

"Sorry, yeah," he nodded. "I know you don't dress like that all the time, and I don't think you plan on doing it all the time or anything. But, I think it looks good. I think it all just makes you look older or more mature or something."

"Yeah, I won't be dressing like this much at all," I assured him. "Tonya kind of went overboard."

"Okay," Peter said after a rather long pause. "Well, see you out there."

"Hey, Peter?" I called as he turned away. Once he turned back I continued. "Thanks."

"Uh, yeah. You're welcome."

Before he turned and left I watched as Peter's cheeks turn red. It took me a minute to realize he was blushing. But that couldn't have been right. Why would a thank you from me cause him to blush? I assumed it must have been because he had gotten too much sun, so I closed my bedroom door and changed into my swimsuit. Hopefully returning to the pool without a dress would help both of my friends start acting like normal.

CHAPTER 18

Despite my hoping that things would be like usual, Peter continued to act oddly around me for the rest of the day and Sunday morning as well. He just stayed quiet while he was acting weird, so I was able to ignore him. Having him constantly staring at me was a little annoying, but thankfully after we swam Sunday morning and had lunch, I had to leave for my pitching clinic. Sitting in the car with my dad on the way to the gymnasium I was suddenly nervous. Not until that moment did I think about the fact that I had my hair now cut short and 'cute,' plus I had bright red polish on my nails.

"Are you okay?" my dad asked as he pulled into the parking lot. Clearly, he was picking up on my nerves.

"I think so," I shrugged. "I just want to do a good job and show people I'm a good catcher."

"You're a great catcher, so just try to have fun in there," he suggested. "You have the skills, you just need to stay calm. Whether you work with a pitcher that is really good or really bad, you're going to do great at catching and that's what's important."

"Thanks, Dad," I said with a smile, giving him a quick hug before climbing out of the air conditioned car and into the hot Texas air.

I walked into the now familiar school gym and checked in at the table just inside the entrance. I once again pinned the number 12 to my shirt, then walked towards the girls that were standing and chatting before the clinic got started. My goal was to be outgoing and try to talk to them first, rather than be annoyed when people didn't go out of their way to say hello to me. But, as I got closer, I instantly knew the plan might not be a successful one.

"Hey," I said to Cate who was talking to a few girls I more or less recognized from the other days of the clinic.

"Hi," she said, taking a long pause to look me over. "You sure look fancy."

"Yeah, I got my hair cut yesterday," I said simply, not bothering to address my nails. "So did you want to work together tonight?"

"I'm already working with Ella," she explained, gesturing to a girl standing next to her.

"Oh, okay." I tried to say the words with a smile, but I got the feeling Cate had chosen to work with Ella on purpose. As in, chose to work with her so she wouldn't have to work with me.

Cate and Ella turned to walk to the other side of the gym then, leaving me alone with the other girls I didn't know. They were all talking to each other with their backs pretty much turned to me, as if to point out the fact that I was not a part of their conversation. When I stepped closer to the two girls, hoping to pause their chatting so I could introduce myself, it took a solid minute for them to get the hint.

"Hey, I'm Max," I said to the girls. They were both quite a bit taller than me, wearing matching green shirts featuring a logo I recognized as of the best teams in town.

"Were you on Diamond Plumbing last year?" one girl asked me, squinting her brown eyes at me. I nodded, kicking myself for not wearing a team shirt like everyone else. "Oh."

And that was it. With the one word, the girls turned their backs on me and went back to talking just like they were before I walked up. I looked at the other dozen or so people around me and realized that if I tried to talk to someone else, I would likely get the same response over and over again. While that was sinking in, I tried to not let it get to me too much. Maybe some of the girls were not talking to me because they were just in important conversations. Or maybe they were just not feeling friendly. Either way, I walked over and put on my catching gear to fill the time. My hope was that once I was in my gear, someone would need me to catch for them. And thankfully, I was right.

"Are you catching for anyone yet?" a girl asked me, approaching with a less than excited look on her face.

"Not yet," I told her with a smile as I pulled the front half of my hair up in a clear hair tie so it would stay out of my face.

"Can you catch for me then?" The words were accompanied with a facial expression that was more or less an eye roll.

Nodding, I followed her down the gymnasium, telling myself over and over again not to take it personally. Like everyone else in the gym around me, the girl I was following was a good bit taller than me. She had on a thick strap tank top that showed off her muscled arms and skin that looked like it was peeling from sunburn on her shoulders. When she turned to me to start pitching I finally got a good look at her face. She had dark brown hair and matching dark brown eyes, along with eyebrows that were thick and made her look like she was giving a constant scowl. Honestly, though, it might have been how she chose to look at me that was causing the real scowl.

Brushing off my worries about how the pitcher might have felt about me, I crouched down and got ready to catch. I balanced my weight on the balls of my feet, allowing my body full range of motion while reaching for the pitch coming my way. I held my mit in a standard strike zone and got ready for the first throw, only to be all but blown away by the pitch that was hurled at me. On top of that, the noise of the ball making contact with my mit was easy to hear around the room. The softball was thrown faster than anyone I had ever caught for before. To say my hand stung from the throw was a bit of an understatement.

In response to the pain in my palm, I mentally took a deep breath and tried to remind myself to keep a level head. I couldn't show anyone that the throw had made my hand hurt. Even though it was a clinic, every coach there was likely going to be watching not only how I caught, but also how I reacted to things like zooming pitches. My hand was numb after a few more balls, so catching got even easier. Or rather the feel of the ball hitting my hand got easier to be used to. The pitches themselves, however, got harder and harder to catch. The pitcher was slowly losing control of the ball. Clearly, she was trying to throw as fast as possible, but it was tiring her arm out just as quickly. The result was unreliable pitches that were only getting worse.

After catching a dozen or so throws that were getting farther and farther from the strike zone, I was starting to get nervous. If I let any of the pitches go by me they were likely going to make a noise when they hit the wall loud enough to stop the rest of the athletes in their tracks. Not to mention it might hurt anyone behind me or at the very least dent the plaster. Her pitching was much worse than Zoe who I caught for on the first night of the clinic. The only difference was that the speed never changed, even as the pitches got more and more crazy. So crazy, in fact, that I finally missed one.

As one particular ball left her hand I could tell it was going to be a low one. Reaching my glove forward, I tried to snag it before it hit the ground. Unfortunately, my reach wasn't far enough and the ball slammed into the gymnasium floor before ricocheting towards me. With my right arm stretched forward, I couldn't pull it back in time to make up for the new path of the ball. So, instead, it continued its extremely fast pace until it made contact with my arm. As if the pain of impact wasn't bad enough on its own, the ball managed to hit my arm in the exact spot of my still healing bruise from cheerleading. And if the loud smack of the ball on my skin wasn't enough to get everyone's attention, I also managed to let out an extremely high pitched yelp thanks to the searing pain.

"Are you okay?" a coach asked, rushing towards me as I dropped to my knees, clutching my right arm.

"I think so," I said, trying hard to blink back tears.

Pulling up my sleeve I could see a perfect red circle, already raising up in a massive welt. It was purple is some parts, but this was from the previous injury. People were walking towards me, but it was hard to see who everyone was with the tears in my eyes. I was mad at myself for even starting to cry, but it felt like the ball didn't just hit my arm. It hit hard enough that the impact made it all the way down to my bone. I took off my glove and tried opening and closing my right hand, feeling my arm throb from the motion. I was relieved when someone reached forward and held an ice pack on my arm. I wasn't sure who placed it there, or even where it came from, but it felt amazing, so I didn't worry or think about it too much.

"Let's get you to the bleachers," a voice suggested from the crowd.

Everyone around me helped to lift me up to my feet then walked with me to the bleachers that were just a few feet away. Once I was sitting down, I looked up and saw that none of the people helping me were the girls that were also at the clinic. All of them were coaches. Glancing behind them, I saw the girls were standing and watching in silence. Or at least everyone aside from Cate. She was talking to some of the girls and mocking me, pretending to cry and acting extra girly with hair flips and everything. It was in that moment that I realized that she had more than likely told the other girls I was a cheerleader before I arrived. Holding the ice to my throbbing bruise, I tried to think how to keep the situation from going from bad to worse. Now it was no longer just about making them see I wasn't being a baby. I also suddenly felt the need to make sure they knew being a cheerleader wasn't a good enough reason to make fun of me. After all, I knew first hand that often the perceptions people had about cheerleaders were far from accurate.

CHAPTER 19

"I think I'm ready to catch again," I said a few minutes later after I had thought about things for a bit. I also used the time to allow my arm to stop throbbing. Or at least stop throbbing quite so much.

"Are ya sure?" a coach asked me. He was a big man, his accent as thick as the brown mustache above his mouth. "Ya took a real hit there, and I dun want ya to get back in there too soon or nuthin'."

"I'll be okay," I assured him, standing up and moving my arm around to stretch it out. Stepping away from the crowd of coaches still near me, I reached my arm over my head in a big stretch. Everyone gave me a little space, just as I hoped. I made a show of rolling my shoulder, and could feel the tightness in my whole arm from the impact the ball had made. That wasn't too important to me though. The important thing in that moment was that I knew everyone had their eyes trained on me. I just needed to use it to my advantage.

Leaning down, I placed my hands on the gym floor then flipped my leg into the air. The handstand felt weird to hold, my arm not quite ready for the strain. But, I knew it was time to get the girls watching me off my back. When Cate heard that I was a cheerleader she wanted nothing to do with me. And sure, I might have reacted the same way a few months ago. But, just like I had needed to learn about all star cheer, she needed to as well. I wanted everyone in the room to know that being an all star cheerleader didn't mean I was anything less than a top-notch athlete.

"Oh my goodness," I heard someone say as I held the handstand in place then slowly lowered myself a few inches closer to the gym floor in what was more or less a push-up. The strain was impossible not to feel, but it was worth it. At the cheer gym I could get a lot closer to the ground, but with the fresh injury, I only managed about half of what I knew I was capable of. Thankfully, it seemed to have its effect.

"Are ya okay?" the mustached coach asked me, not moving towards me even after I was standing back on my feet.

"I think so," I said with a casual shrug. "Just making sure I can still put weight on it."

Before anyone could say or do anything else, I took a step forward and did a roundoff. I hopped in the air after the move, looking towards Cate as I did. Her mouth was open a little in what I assumed was shock. Ella was standing next to her, her eyes nice and wide. With a smile, I took another step forward to try the round off once again. This time, as my feet hit the gym floor I pushed off again, doing a back handspring before ending with a full.

"Yep, I'm okay," I said to the coach who had just asked. Then, with a bit of a skip to my step, I walked over and picked up my mit.

There was a pause in the room as I moved back to stand at the end of the taped off lane where I had been catching. No one seemed to know what to do, but I just played it all off like it was no big deal. The truth was that I was still in a good bit of pain. I knew I would need to apply a lot of IcyHot to my arm before I hit the mat at the TNT gym next time. But I wasn't going to let everyone else know that. I wanted them to see I was tough. After all, cheerleading wasn't a sport just anyone could do.

"Why don't ya try catching for sum wun else for a bit," the same coach said to me, holding his hand out for me to shake. "I'm Nick Varlee. I coach Varlee's Construction."

"That's a great team," I told him, remembering hearing how well they did the previous season. Everyone in town, even in the younger league, knew of the team thanks to their winning record.

"Now my daughter ain't here right now, but I'd like ta see ya catch fer someone with a bit less of a challenge," he drawled.

It was hard to decipher what he was saying through his accent, but I had a feeling it was important, so I focused as best I could. He continued to tell me about his daughter, who was apparently at the last days of clinics that I had also attended. I didn't know her by name, but Coach Varlee assured me that Melanie was a great pitcher. He told me that she was going to be his team's main pitcher now that another girl on the team went on to play for her high school. I nodded, not quite sure where the story was going.

"Here ya go," he bellowed with a grin after a girl he motioned for started walking our way. "I want ya to catch with Amber here. She's tha best we got other than my Melanie. Ya can catch fer her a bit so we can all see what ya got."

With a nod, I gave Melanie a wave then got to work catching. It was a lot easier than catching for the other pitcher, whose name I still didn't know. Not only did Amber throw at a speed that didn't make my catching hand numb, she also could land all her pitches in the strike zone. No matter how many pitches she threw my way, they were accurate every time. Even still, Coach Varlee went and made suggestions to her a few times here and there. Based on the exasperated look on her face, I got the idea that she was sick of his comments. I didn't know how good Melanie was, but Amber was clearly great. Sadly, she would likely always be second best on Varlee's Construction. Or at least only second best in the eyes of the coach who also had his daughter on his team roster.

By the time the clinic was over that evening I was feeling great about everything. I was catching for Amber long enough for my arm to pretty much stop hurting when I threw the ball back her way and got to watch with a smile as the new catcher working with my previous pitcher struggled. Ball after the ball made it past her, hopefully showing that I had worked hard to catch everything but the last ball thrown my way. I took off my catching gear after we were finally done and headed towards the exit when I heard Coach Varlee call for me.

"Number 12?" he called out, causing me to turn his way. "Ya have a second?"

"Sure," I replied easily, knowing my dad wouldn't mind waiting.

"Ya got talent," Coach Varlee began with a grin. "That catching fer Courtney was hard work, and ya did it. Ya did real good the whole time. Even when that ball hit ya arm, ya were tough as nails. That shows what yer made of."

"Thanks." I didn't know what else to say but was as least happy to know the name of the pitcher that caused my arm to still be in pain.

"Now like I said, my lil girl Amber ain't here right now," he went on finally. "She had another commitment, so didn't make it like I asked. But, she gunna be here fer the last clinic, and I wanna to see ya catch fer her. Yous all sorts of tiny, but ya got a lot of heart ta keep going after that hit and the way ya caught fer Courtney fer so long. If yer as good a catcher fer Amber as ya were catching today, then I think yous got a spot on my team this season."

"That would be great," my reply came easily. "I'd love to catch for her."

"Perfect," he drawled. "I'll see ya at the next clinic then darlin'."

And with that, he walked away from me, towards where a few other coaches were standing. They were all watching me, I noticed. Sure, it could have been that they were just seeing what Coach Varlee was talking to me about. But, I also got the feeling they were discussing my show of cheerleading moves. This dawned on me as I walked towards the door and was stopped by Cate.

"What was that you did earlier?" Cate asked, Ella by her side.

"My catching?" I asked although I knew what she was referring to.

"No the flips and stuff you did," she tried again.

"Oh that," I said with a shrug. "It was just some basic cheerleading stuff to test my arm. I have a big international competition coming up and wanted to make sure I could handle putting weight on my arm with the new bruise."

"Is it already purple?" Ella asked, pointing to the older bruise peeking out below my shirts hem.

"Not all of it," I explained, pulling up my sleeve and rotating my arm so both bruises were visible. "I got this one when my stunt team dropped me a few days ago."

"Dropped you?"

"Yeah," I said in reply to Ella's question. "I'm a flier so I get picked up and held above the mat by other girls on my team."

"Oh," Cate said, not really understanding.

"Here, I have a photo." Pulling out my phone I showed the two girls a photo where I was being held up by my stunt team. I was doing a bow and arrow in the photo. My left leg was held next to my head using my right hand and my left arm was crossing over the leg. The move was one I could hold easily for a long time, but I knew it looked cool in photos.

"Wow," Ella managed, glancing at Cate as if for approval.

"That's cool," Cate confirmed.

"Thanks," I said honestly, glad to have impressed both of them. "Well, I should go."

The girls muttered some kind of reply, but at that point, I was flying too high to even listen. I walked outside and had a genuine grin on my face as I climbed into my dad's car. He asked me about my arm, having seen the now much larger bruise as I buckled my seatbelt. I explained the injury through my smile, despite the discomfort the bruise was still giving me. Finally, my mood being too much to ignore, he asked what I was so happy about.

"The coach from Varlee's Construction wants to see me catch for his daughter at the next clinic," I explained in a rush. "I think he wants me to be on his team."

"That's amazing sweetie." He paused then, before adding the words that wiped away my smile in seconds. "But how can you go to the next clinic if you're in Florida for Summit?"

CHAPTER 20

I'm not sure why I didn't remember about Summit until my dad brought it up, but that was the only thing I really thought about the rest of the night. I sat at the table and worked on homework while icing my new bruise, and went over everything in my head. The clinic was going to be held on Tuesday, which was my day in Florida to spend with Halley and Lexi. It meant that in order to go to the clinic I would have to arrive Wednesday, and not only miss the time with my friends but also the first day of practice. And it wasn't just Blast that would be affected if I arrived late.

The girls on Fuze would also be missing me for running stunts and skills as well.

I was so focused on thinking things over I basically ignored my phone the rest of the weekend, as well as most of the beginning of the week. The idea of starting a conversation that might lead to someone bringing up softball, Summit, or anything in between was not something I was at all interested in. I was a little worried that my friends would be annoyed with me for not talking to them, but that thought was instantly wiped from my head when I walked into the gym for Blast practice on Tuesday night. As soon as everyone saw my hair, it was all they could talk about!

"I can't believe you didn't snapchat me!" Lexi exclaimed, actually jumping up and down with excitement.

"Sorry," I managed between other people making comments about my hair. "I had a lot of homework to do so I was kind of distracted."

"That's okay," she gushed. "But now I totally want to go back to short hair too!"

As Lexi, Halley, and the other girls went on and on about my hair as well as my nails, I looked around the gym and realized it was empty aside from the ladies of Blast. It hit me then that most of the teams were already either in Florida or were on their way there for Worlds. Realizing that we were the only team at the gym for practice was both a relief and weird at the same time. I knew if more people were there then it would mean more people would be going on and on about my hair. But, at the same time, the lack of people also meant that no one was going to be there to cheer us on while we practiced. And in that moment, I wondered if we would still be able to hit as many full outs as we were hoping for.

"Did you sent Connor a picture of your hair?" Halley asked then, making the whole group of girls around me quiet down instantly.

"Uh, no," I said in reply. "But I can, I guess."

"No!" someone yelled, catching me off guard.

"Yeah, make him wait to see you in person," Anna suggested, a grin plastered on her face.

"Okay," I said slowly, making it sound like more of a question.

"If you snapchat him between now and then don't let him see your hair, okay?" Lexi explained. "He is going to be in shock when he sees it Monday."

The mention of Monday had me thinking about the softball clinic immediately.

As Nicole told us to line up for warmups, I started thinking again about whether or not I should try to head to Summit late. If I chose to go on time with everyone else, then I would be arriving in Florida on Monday night around 7pm. It would mean I would see all of the Worlds teams before most of them headed home on Tuesday morning. Some athletes were staying all week, but I knew Connor was flying out Tuesday afternoon. If I decided to do the softball clinic I wouldn't be able to fly out at all until either super late Tuesday or super early Wednesday. It would mean I would miss team practices, and also a chance to see Connor and hopefully congratulate him on winning Worlds. He was one of my best friends at the gym, and the idea of not getting to see him before I took the stage at Summit was a little weird.

"Where's the energy ladies?" Nicole called out as we began running different sections of the routine once warm-ups were over. "I know we don't have as many people here tonight, but I need to see you all performing start to finish."

I couldn't help but notice Nicole was looking at me as she spoke those words. With my thoughts on softball and Summit and even Connor, I knew I wasn't performing like I was capable of. Trying to push the other things from my mind, I focused on the routine and the little things like facial expressions and attitude. As a flier, it was my job to really sell the routine at different times. Hand gestures and smiles needed to be over the top. And when I was high above the mat holding a stunt, I needed to look like it was the greatest thing in the world. I could always tell whether or not I had done a good job on all of that by the end of practice. If my face hurt from the over the top smiles and facial expressions, then it meant that I did a good job. Knowing I couldn't make a decision one way or the other about softball just then, I set my mind to reach that sore face point!

By the time we took a break less than an hour later my face was feeling the burn a lot. I was proud of that fact, but also not enjoying the feeling at the same time. Using my hands to rub my cheek muscles, I grabbed my water bottle and phone out of my cheer bag. Pulling up my notifications I wasn't too surprised to see a lot of missed messages from Connor. Since I couldn't be there to see him at Worlds he was sending me information about everything so I felt like I was still a part of everything. Most of his snaps were also posted to his snapchat story, but there were also quite a few photos and videos that were only sent my way. Wanting to reply, I started to take a selfie, only to have Lexi grab my phone from my hands.

"You can't message Connor," she reminded me.

"But he sent me a bunch of stuff," I told her with a sigh. "Can't I just sent a photo without my hair in the picture?"

"Fine, but I get to be in it!" she finally decided.

I couldn't help but laugh at Lexi for that one, but leaned in closer to her for a picture all the same. She held the phone at a weird angle that showed mostly her, and only the bottom half of my face. Since my hair was in a half ponytail, held in place by my bow, Lexi made sure that it didn't show in the photo. She also added a caption to let Connor know that she was the one that took the photo. Eventually, I would be sending him photos when I wasn't with her, but I didn't bring it up in that moment. The idea of letting him see my hair in person was fun enough that I decided I would try to keep selfies 'safe,' like Lexi and the other girls encouraged.

"Who's ready to beat our full out record?" Nicole asked, ending the water break before I could worry about sending any more snapchats to Connor.

Standing up, I tossed my phone into my bag and walked to my spot on the mat. It was going to a take a lot for me to stay focused on the routine and not think about all the other things that had been on my mind lately. But, with a deep breath, I tried to push everything out of my head aside from the routine. Plastering a big smile on my face, I counted along in my head to the music then launched into my first series of skills and tumbling.

CHAPTER 21

After Blast and Fuse practice Tuesday night it felt like time was dragging. With no reason to go to the gym, it was like I had too much free time. On top of that I was wrestling with my decision to skip part of Summit still, so talking to my friends made me nervous. I was always afraid I was going to say the wrong thing. When I finally walked into Blast practice Thursday night, everyone was worried something was going on with me. I went through the motions of the routine more or less like usual, but it was hard to ignore the questions and worried looks my friends were sending my way. Once I got home from practice, the questions continued, this time in text form. I tried, again and again, to tell them I was fine, but no one appeared to be buying it. Even Nicole seemed to notice something was up since as soon as I walked into Fuze practice on Friday she pulled me aside to talk.

"How are you doing Max?" she asked immediately. The other girls on Fuze were stretching on the blue mat a few feet from us. A few feet out of earshot thankfully.

"Good," I said automatically, hoping to end the conversation.

"Max, what's going on?" This time, her words were different. Her voice was filled with so much caring and concern that I was shocked for a second. I had seen Nicole as a coach, but never a friend, like I did Tonya after our moment during TNT Force Camp right after I joined the gym. Tonya was there for me in such a big way when I felt like I would never fit in with other cheerleaders. Nicole, on the other hand, always seemed to have a wall in place. Her voice told me that wall was coming down, and she was really worried about me.

"I just have a lot on my mind." It felt like the safe thing to say.

"Can I ask," Nicole began slowly, as if doubting her words even as she said them. "Is this about your mom?"

Bringing up my mom in that moment was not what I expected. I stared at Nicole, feeling my heart constricting in my chest suddenly. Sure, I wasn't upset at that moment because my mom was dead, but hearing Nicole bring it up was like a punch to the gut. It had been a little while since I felt it so strongly, even though there were constant memories every day. After the ache in my chest subsided, I realized I needed to clear things up. I had bad days where missing her was all I could think about, but to lie and say that it was the cause of why I was in a less than happy mood didn't feel right.

"It's softball," I finally admitted. "There's a coach for a really good team that wants to see me catch for his daughter at the next pitching clinic. It's the last one before tryouts, so it's my chance to really show him what I've got."

"That's nothing to worry about," she said with a smile. "Based on what your dad was telling me you're even better at softball than you are at cheer. And that's saying a lot."

"I'm not worried about doing well," I went on before I could chicken out. "I'm kind of worried because the last clinic is on Tuesday. If I want to go to the clinic, then I need to go late to Summit. I wouldn't be able to get there until later in the day on Wednesday."

After I spoke it was silent between Nicole and myself. She pursed her lips, and in that moment I could tell she was deep in thought. But, what I didn't know was what she was thinking. Was she about to tell me she was disappointed in me? Was she about to tell me to skip Summit? Was she even going to talk? It felt like an hour passed before she spoke to me finally.

"I understand your worries, Max," she began at last. "You're still new here to the gym, and I know you used to play a lot of other sports. I think that's what keeps you going and pushing. You have a competitive drive that I haven't seen in a lot of other athletes so soon after them joining the gym. But I guess I shouldn't be surprised that you still want to participate in other sports." She paused, thinking and choosing her words once again. "I can't make you be there for those first few days at Summit. I honestly think you will be fine to get on the stage and perform without attending the practices on Wednesday. You're a great athlete, and I have all the confidence in you. But what I'm worried about is all of them."

I turned with Nicole and looked at the girls on the mat. The girls in purple practice uniforms were stretching, chatting, and getting ready for the two hours of workouts to follow. There were only a few girls on the team I would call friends since I was used to spending all of my time with Blast or the athletes in my stunt class. But, looking at them, I knew what Nicole meant. They were counting on me. And not just them. All my friends on Blast were counting on me as well.

"We have some athletes at this gym that have been dreaming of going to Summit for years," Nicole continued. "Girls that had been so close so many years, and are only just now finally getting to go. Not to mention the girls that leave after this year. We have 4 girls on Fuze that won't be cheering with us after this season. For them, Summit will be their last performance with the TNT. So when I think about you missing even a second of the time leading up to Summit I wonder what they will say."

"Do they have to know?" I asked, the words slipping out before I realized I wasn't just saying them in my head.

"I think so," she said slowly with a nod. "I guess that's it really. If you can take the time tonight and let Fuze know, and then find a time to let Blast know, then the choice will be up to you. The girls might be mad, or upset, or maybe they won't mind. But if you can stand there and tell them everything, then the choice will be yours to decide. I can't force you to be in Florida on Monday night as planned. I also can't be upset at you for wanting to do softball.

You are important to us here at the gym, but you are more than just a person on a team. We care about how you feel, and whether or not you are happy as well. And if you miss a little of Summit, we can only be thankful that we have you here as a part of the gym family for the stuff that's important."

Nicole's words weighed heavy on me as I began practice with Fuze. Juleah, Petin, and Erin kept me in the air for every stunt, I landed in the right spot for every tumbling pass and managed to get every dance move right all evening. Somehow, I even managed to keep a smile on my face while performing to make it all look how it would on the stage at Summit. But, behind my smile, I was freaking out. Could I really tell these girls that I was going to miss out on a part of Summit for a chance to play on a team? That I was going to miss important practice time in hopes of impressing a coach that I only met once? How would they react to me putting cheerleading second to softball, during the biggest competition of the year for their team? How was I going to tell them, and then still have the guts to tell my teammates on Blast as well?

As the practice finally ended, we circled up and sat on the mat while drinking from our water bottles. Looking around I saw that every girl looked the same in so many ways. We all had on our black tank tops with the glittery purple TNT logo, purple shorts, and of course our purple ombre cheer bow in our hair. Everyone wore the same cheer shoes, drank from the same water bottle, and had the same cheer bag waiting in their cubbies. It was odd to think how different we looked and acted than any other team I had been on. At soccer, basketball, or baseball we would dress alike for games. But those practices were always just no big deal. At those practices, I would work hard, try to work well with my team, and then go home. Even after three years living in Texas, I didn't have a lot of people I felt close to on other team sports. But at cheer, I walked in and was welcomed. After a few weeks of struggling to fit in, I realized that people cared about me. I had gained so many friends on Blast, and even though I was new, the girls on Fuze were genuinely excited to see me and practice with me every week. The idea of having to stand up and tell them that softball was more important than getting ready for a massive competition like Summit was the last thing in the world I wanted to do in that moment.

Nicole was telling us about leaving for Florida, what to expect when we got there, and also going over some important reminders before travel. It was not our first out of state competition of the season, but it was the farthest away trip yet, so she wanted to make sure we were all really ready. Although e-mails had been sent out days prior, she went over everything one more time. I knew part of this was likely because some of the older girls on the squad wouldn't have their parents there for the competition.

"Does anyone want to add anything?" Nicole finally asked after she was done with the important information. Georgina and Liz, the two team captains, gave a quick word about getting rest, then there was silence on the mat.

Nicole's eyes landed on me, but I kept my face a mask. I knew right then that I wasn't going to speak up. From that moment on I just needed to focus on cheer while I could, and worry about softball later. Too many people were counting on me at the TNT Force gym. Some of the girls around me eventually shared how happy they were for the competition, or gave tips about travel or about things for once we got to Florida. I took it all in, trying to focus on the girls around me and getting excited about the trip. Softball was off the table, so it was time I focused all in on cheer.

"Does this mean you're still planning to arrive on time for Summit?" Nicole asked me as I was finally walking out of the gym a few minutes later.

"Yeah," I nodded. "Are you going to tell anyone that I was thinking about missing for softball?"

"No," Nicole assured me. "Not unless you want people to know."

"Maybe one day," I said with a shrug. "But for now, I'm just trying to focus on getting to Summit and doing a good job with my teams."

Nicole smiled and let me know that my secret was safe with her. And, as I walked away from her, I finally felt good about Summit. Really and truly good. Before then it was like Summit was something I didn't think my teams were ready for, or it felt like something I didn't want to go to if it meant I wasn't going to get to be on a good softball team. But, as I walked with my dad out of the gym I realized that I was going to be competing against the best teams in the world. Not just on one team, but two. Finally accepting everything was making me think less and less about softball. Instead, I could just focus on trying to see the positive in leaving for Summit on Monday with my best friends. I may miss out on a team for softball, but having finally made a decision was a bigger relief than I thought it would be.

CHAPTER 22

Although my dad had told me that the decision as to when we left for Summit was my choice, when I gave him the news after practice on Friday, he was excited, to say the least. I think part of it was because he and the other parents had been planning a treat for all the athletes, and handing out gifts or things to the athletes was always his favorite. For example, on my birthday back in January, my dad got everyone in the gym Happy Birthday Max bows to wear to practice. There was of course also cake for everyone as well, but his real pride and joy was ordering all the matching bows for the girls at the gym. Oh, and he got all the guys birthday trucker hats so they didn't feel too left out. I thought it was a bit much, but it was all anyone could talk about for a solid week.

"I want you packed and ready to go tomorrow night before you go to bed," my dad told me Saturday morning as we sat folding laundry. It was raining outside, so for once I didn't mind helping with the housework.

"Okay," I nodded, knowing I would likely get it done well before then.

Picking up a sock from the basket of clothing, I was met with resistance. Looking down I realized that while I was absentmindedly folding socks and watching TV, Storm had climbed into the basket and was having a fun time jumping around and chewing on items. He held the other end of the sock in his mouth and was batting at it with his paws. Lightning was across the room sleeping on his cat bed, so thankfully I only had one kitten to battle for the sock.

"What are we going to do with these guys while we're gone?" I asked, rubbing the kitten's belly as a distraction so I could take the sock from him easily.

"Peter and Kyle said they're going to come over a few times and check their food and water," Dad explained between folding beach towels.

"You mean they'll come over and make sure the cats are okay then spend a few hours playing video games on the big screen TV?"

"Janet said she will come over with them," Dad said with a laugh, knowing I was right.

The best part about having me for a neighbor, aside from our pool, was that we had a massive TV and every video game imaginable in the basement rec room. I didn't use the games all the time, but Peter and Kyle more than made up for it when they came over. Hopefully, with their mom joining them to check on the cats they would stay focused and not spend too much time playing around.

The sound of my phone alarm going off got me flying up from the couch immediately. My dad, knowing it was a 'Worlds alarm,' just took over sorting socks for me as I raced down the hall to my room. Leaping across my bed, I picked up my laptop and began powering it up. While it booted up I texted Lexi and Halley to make sure they were also watching. Then, once I finally got the screen loaded and entered my password I was greeted with the live feed from the stage at the World Cheerleading Competition. There was a team on the screen performing, and after checking the schedule I had still pulled up on my browsers, I saw that Nitro would be taking the stage in just a few minutes.

"Max?" I heard a voice call out as steps in the hallway neared my room. Recognizing Peter's voice, I rolled my eyes and let out a sigh. I was instantly annoyed that he was just going to sit and stare at me again, making it so I couldn't even enjoy watching Connor and the other athletes perform.

"In my room," I said, although he was clearly heading that way already.

"Wanna go to the movies?" Peter asked me, plopping onto the bed next to me, not even caring that the move made my laptop jostle around. I was laying down flat on my stomach and thankfully was able to hold it in place before it bounced off my bed completely.

"No," I said, letting out a sigh as I released my grip on the computer to text Lexi who was sending me lots of smiling emoji's.

"What are you doing?" he asked as if finally paying attention to me and my laptop.

"Watching cheer," I said shortly without taking my eyes off my phone.

"So watch it later," he replied.

"I'm watching Words," I tried again. When he didn't respond to that I went on. "A few of the teams from my gym are performing this weekend in Florida and I want to watch them on the live feed. Connor's team is about to go any minute now. He said he was going to message me when he's off the stage, but I want to actually see everything in real time."

"Oh goody."

Peter's tone was less than happy as he turned to flop down onto my bed so he was resting his head on my pillows. He turned to me, his face partly blocked by my computer. I ignored him, instead focusing on the screen that was showing the last team performing before Nitro. As they finished I hopped up to sit on my knees, no longer able to contain my building excitement.

Watching Nitro as they came out onto the stage, I spotted Connor right away. He was front and center as they got in place for the jump sequence that started the routine. I took a photo of my computer and sent it to his snapchat so he could see it when he checked his phone. Since Matthew was also on stage I sent him the photo as well, knowing it would be fun for him to see. Then, as the team began performing I found myself cheering as if I was in front of the stage with the other athletes from the gym. I screamed and hopped up and down on my bed when stunts landed, I yelled "hit" for their jumps, and even clapped along to the dance section that ended the routine.

Finally, once they held their final poses I jumped up off my bed and hopped in place while cheering! Aside from one small stunt bobble they performed a perfect routine, all but ensuring that they would make it to the next day of competition.

"Are you done yet?" Peter asked, startling me. For a minute I forgot he was even in my room.

Turning away from him I took a photo of myself with a massive smile on my face and sent it to Halley, Lexi, and Connor on snapchat. I did my best to not show all of my hair, mostly to avoid the wrath of my friends. I also took a selfie so my computer could be seen in the background, but when I saw the grumpy look on Peter's face I deleted it before I could send it out.

"So, are you done?" he asked again.

Shooting him a glare I sat back at my computer and checked to see what team was on stage. They weren't in Nitro's division, so I wasn't too interested. I knew it would be a few more hours until Gwen and the other athletes on Bomb Squad would be performing, so I closed the laptop and finally looked at Peter.

"You're annoying," I said to him, not sure how else to express myself other than stating the truth. "Worlds is going on, so I need to stay here to watch updates."

"Seriously?" he asked. "You're really going to not do anything all day just to find out how people do? Can't you like just check after it's over?"

"Yes," I nodded. "But I'm not going to. I have to pack for Summit today and finish a paper for English that's due while I'm gone. Even if I didn't have all that, I would want to stay home to watch Worlds. It's bad enough I'll probably be in the air during the finals and won't find out if Nitro wins until I land Monday night."

"What about the other teams at your gym? You don't care if they win?"

"I care," I assured him. "I'm watching their routines too. Connor is one of my best friends though, so I especially need to show support for him."

Peter rolled his eyes then stood up from my bed. When he made it the door he turned around and leaned on the door frame. I waited, but when he didn't do or say anything I sat down on my blue comforter and looked at my phone. Lexi was sending me snapchat responses, and Halley was sending me every emoji she could to express her excitement. Hearing Peter clear his throat, I looked up from my phone just as a new text came in from Skyler who had also just watched Nitro perform.

"What?" I asked with a sigh. "Can't I just watch cheer and stay home if I want to?"

"I guess," Peter said slowly. "I just wanted to hang out with you before you leave for Florida."

The lack of attitude in his tone had me confused. It sounded like he was being sincere. I set my phone down and looked at him, waiting for him to say more. When he didn't I finally spoke.

"Why didn't you come over all this week if you wanted to hang out with me?"

"I had stuff I was doing," he shrugged. "But I'm free today and I thought we could go see a movie or something."

"Well, I have stuff going on here," I said, waving my arm through the air as if pointing out my clean room made it obvious. "You can hang out, but I'm going to be watching cheer a lot. And I'm going to be texting people about Worlds too. It's kind of take it or leave it."

I waited, expecting him to walk out or make a comment about how stupid watching everything live was. But instead, he simply pulled out his phone. He sent a text, that I could only assume was to let either Kyle or his

226

parents know he was staying at my house, then stood up from his leaning position and rubbed his hands together.

"Okay, how do you need me to help?"

"How are you at folding socks?" I asked with a smile, getting up and walking past him into the living room where my dad still sat surrounded by clean clothes.

CHAPTER 23

     Lying in bed Sunday night I passed the time by staring at the ceiling, trying my hardest not to look at my phone. I had been laying there awake for what felt like hours, my body refusing to fall asleep. The excitement of leaving for Summit in the morning was just too much for me to ignore. Watching the live feed from Worlds all day Saturday and Sunday didn't help. In fact, I think it made it worse.

     At first, Peter would more or less ignore me when I opened my computer to watch a routine on Saturday. But, by the end of the day, he started watching them right along with me. It wasn't until I mentioned that Nitro's division was done performing though, that I had to watch by myself as I found out Connor and his team were in 4th place. Even the one small bobble was enough to keep them from the top spots, thanks to a lot of the other teams with hard skills in their routines. It wasn't that Nitro was a bad team, they were just up against hard teams.

When I mentioned all of that to Connor, it hit home for me too. There was no guarantee Blast was going to make it to the finals of Summit. Even with a harder routine, it wasn't a sure thing. Fuze was also not a shoo-in, even after coming in first or second all season. Apparently, I wasn't the only one thinking about Summit the whole time I was watching Worlds, since every time I watched a routine from our gym or a team I knew we were up against, I would get lots of texts from my friends. Even Connor took the time to message me frequent updates once he was done performing for the day and had a little more time on his hands.

"Can't wait to see you when you get here tomorrow!" Connor texted me as I was getting ready for bed Sunday night. "Hopefully, you being on the way here will be the luck we need to come in first."

"You don't need any luck," I wrote in reply. "You hit today, and were almost perfect yesterday! You keep it up and those Worlds rings are all yours."

Connor and I chatted a little longer, but even once we stopped talking so he could get some sleep, I was wide awake. I wasn't sure if it was the mention of the next day or even the anticipation of hopefully winning Summit that got to me. Whatever it was, I couldn't get my brain to shut down and let me sleep. All I could think about was heading to Florida, finding out how all the TNT teams did at Worlds, and then, of course, compete at Summit. Well, that and softball. I got a direct message from Hillary on Instagram just before bed asking me if I was going to the clinic. She hadn't been at the others since she isn't a pitcher but was going to the final one to help her mom who would be running the check-in table. When I told her I was going to be in Florida for cheer stuff she just said "bummer" and that was the end of it. The fact that she didn't say "well I'm sure you're still going to get on a good team" or anything like that had me worried.

I hoped that worrying about things would tire me out and I would fall asleep, but I still felt like I hadn't gotten a second of rest when my dad's alarm went off at 6 am. I didn't need to be awake that early since we weren't leaving for the airport until 9. But, by that point, I figured I might as well get up and get moving. It was better than just lying there with all kinds of thoughts, worries, and excitements going through my mind.

"You're up early," my dad grinned as I walked into the kitchen a minute later. He was already dressed in jeans and his 'CHEER DAD' shirt, this one purple in honor of Fuze.

I managed some form of a mumbled reply as I sat down at the kitchen table and pulled my knees up to my chest. Resting my head on my knees I could hear either Storm or Lightning purring and meowing at my feet. When I didn't reach down to pet them I could feel them trying to climb up the chair without success. So, with a heavy sigh, I placed my feet on the ground and picked up what turned out to be Lightning and placed him on my lap. Storm was nowhere in sight, but I knew he would likely be running around before too long.

"You doing okay sweetie?" My dad was making coffee and getting out ingredients to make breakfast. "Did you sleep okay?"

"No," I said in answer to both questions at the same time. "I don't think I ever really fell asleep."

"Too excited?" I shrugged in reply to his question. "Well, hopefully you can get some sleep on the flights."

Going back to giving Lightning some attention I was distracted when I heard my phone buzzing from my nightstand. I knew it wasn't my alarm, so figured it would be one of my teammates that was likely also awake. Carrying my cat with me, I walked to my room and picked up my phone, surprised to see it was a text from Connor.

"Sorry if this is super early but I can't remember what time your flight is and wanted to message you before you took off. Have a great time traveling today and I can't wait to see you when you get here. Hopefully we can celebrate a Nitro win together tonight!"

Surprisingly, getting the text from him made me look forward to the day and forget the fact that I hadn't slept at all for the time being. I wrote back, then once he got over the fact I was awake so early we chatted about how Worlds was going for him. It was nice to just sit and talk to him to start my day. I didn't realize it until then that I talked to and saw Connor a few times a week ever since I started at the gym. Just like Halley, Lexi, Peter, and Kyle, Connor really was one of my best friends. So, after over a week with only a few texts or snapchats a day, having a real conversation with him was really nice.

I talked to Connor for a lot longer than I planned to, so when breakfast was ready I ate quickly then got dressed for the airport. Nicole let everyone know that we were expected to represent the gym from the second we checked in for our flights, so I wore jeans and my black TNT Force short sleeve shirt. I heard a few girls talking about how we would get new shirts and even bows once we got to Florida, but for the time being the team shirt worked just fine for me. Packing up the last of my carry-on items, I was in the car and headed to the airport right on time at 9 am. Just as, of course, the texts began from Lexi and Halley, who were also on their way to the airport.

"Aren't you going to see them soon enough?" my dad asked after we pulled out of the driveway.

"No," I shrugged with a laugh. "Halley's mom had to stop at the store for something so I won't see her for at least 15 minutes."

"And Lexi?" he asked in a serious tone, despite the smile on his face.

"She's waiting at the airport door so we can go through check in together."

In reply, my dad just laughed and continued driving. The airport was just across town so we were there in a matter of minutes. As I climbed out of the car and walked to the main entrance, Lexi ran and hugged me, jumping up and down with excitement. I was still tired, but seeing her had me more than excited for Summit. Sure, we had a few hours of flight ahead of us, but it was all finally happening. We, of course, waited impatiently at the doors for Halley, greeting her the same way Lexi greeted me, then made our way through security.

We spotted a few other girls from our gym when we got to our gate, although most of them were on other teams. I recognized two girls from Fuze, so I gave them a wave before we sat down. Most of the other athletes would either be leaving later in the day or first thing Tuesday morning so the airport wasn't quite as packed with TNT cheerleaders as I thought it might have been. I only had a second to notice this before Lexi and Halley began grilling me on my appearance.

"You're putting on makeup, right?" Halley asked as soon as we were sitting down with a bit of space between ourselves and our parents.

"And you're going to do your hair, right?" Lexi also chimed in.

"No," I said with a shake of my head. "Why would I?"

"It's your hair," Lexi said simply. When my only reply was a shrug she continued. "Your hair is awesome now, and you need to look super cute when you see everyone."

"You mean Connor?" Halley asked, causing both girls to giggle.

"I really don't care what I look like," I said with an overly dramatic roll of my eyes for effect.

"As your best friends we will hold you down and do your hair and makeup if we have to," Lexi assured me. "You have to look cute for when we get to Florida. Trust me."

"I don't want to wear makeup all day," I tried, hoping that if I made them forget about it for a little while, they would drop the issue altogether.

"Okay," Halley nodded. "We can do your hair during the layover in Dallas and then we can do your makeup on the flight into Orlando."

"Fine," I said with a sigh, praying that by the time we were in Dallas they wouldn't even remember their plans to ambush me. I had a feeling they would remember at all costs. But, a girl could still dream, right?

CHAPTER 24

"Stop. No glitter," I whined as Lexi began applying eyeshadow to my face. I already had on a thin layer of foundation and a light pink blush that she had assured me wasn't too dramatic.

"It's not glitter," she said with a frown. "It's a normal shade with an iridescent shimmer."

With yet another sigh, I closed my eyes as she began applying the shadow to my eyelids. I wanted to complain, but she was thankfully using a gold color that wasn't as over the top as I initially feared. Knowing all three of us had bright red glitter and eyeshadow in our makeup bags, I was assuming I would be coated in something similar to our team makeup we wore on the mat. But, between applications of the shadow, I saw that she was using a light gold, a medium brown color, and then a little bit of a light purple. The purple seemed odd to me, but when I asked about it, she just told me to stop worrying.

While Lexi was finishing my makeup with what she assured me was a thin line of eyeliner and a few layers of mascara, Halley was straightening my hair and putting it up in a half ponytail with a mini poof in front to look "cute, but not over the top." Although my hair was mostly straightened when we were in the airport, when she saw there was a plug at our seats on the plane she decided to touch it up just in case. I felt a little silly sitting there getting a makeover on the flight, but the flight attendants and other cheerleaders we knew sitting around us thought it was great. Everyone kept assuring me I looked amazing and kept encouraging Lexi and Halley to keep going. But, I reminded them, I was still drawing the line at glitter.

"Okay, all done," Lexi told me with a massive grin after applying one last layer of mascara. Halley had been done with my hair for a while since it was mostly finished when we boarded the flight. "Want to see?"

"Fine," I said slowly. But, when Lexi held up a mirror I was shocked. "What did you do to my eyes?"

"Do you like?" Lexi asked, moving her eyebrows up and down at the grin that was quickly growing on my face.

"They look super blue," I said, not used to seeing my eyes surrounded by any eyeshadow colors other than silver, red, and most recently purple.

"Golds and purples go well with your eye color," she explained. As I opened my mouth to explain that I had tried purple eye makeup for Fuze she added, "This shade of purple, I should say."

Pulling the mirror back a little I was surprised to see how good my hair looked as well. I had done a front poof a few times to practice, but not the way Halley managed. It wasn't as big as it would be for a competition, but was perfect to wear day to day. I made the mental note to try it out and do my hair that way more often for school. So, as I finally handed the mirror to Lexi and sat back in my seat, I had to admit how great everything looked.

"This is awesome," I told them both. "I thought you were going to make me look like I was going to a competition."

"Ew no," Halley said with a shake of her head. "Do I look like I'm wearing competition makeup?"

"You're wearing makeup?" I asked, instantly feeling bad. "Wait. I didn't mean-"

"It's okay," she assured me. "Do enough to make it look nice but still natural. I'm only wearing foundation and powder and blush and bronzer. And of course a little mascara."

"Me too," Lexi added. "Only no bronzer. My mom doesn't like when I go overboard for school and stuff like that. She said I can wear more makeup once I'm actually a teenager. Kind of annoying."

"I really didn't think you guys were wearing anything," I said with a shrug. "You look like this at practice, so I just assumed it was natural."

"I mean, I don't wear much," Lexi said. "But I wear it all the time. Even to practice."

"Me too. Although I skip the blush and bronzer for practice. I just always have to have something on my face to keep from sweating too much," Halley chimed in.

As the girls started going back and forth about different makeups they tried for a certain week of cheer, or one they wanted to get, and other things of that nature, I just sat back and snuck another peek of myself in my phone's

240

selfie camera. Lexi checked to make sure I wasn't posting to my snapchat story with my new look, but once she was certain I wasn't she went back to her conversation. Much like the first time I put on my cheer makeup, it was just a lot to take in. It looked really great. I just wasn't sure in that moment if I would actually wear makeup to practice or even to school like my friends, but it was fun for Summit. Or at least the first day of Summit. The idea of worrying about whether or not my eyeliner was smudging during a whole team practice would drive me insane!

By the time we landed you couldn't tell that I had slept poorly. Sure, I got a little bit of sleep on the first flight, but not enough to make up for the sudden energy burst I got when we landed. It was like just being that much closer to the Summit stage had me fidgeting while we waited to de-board the plane, and then again while we were waiting for our luggage at baggage claim. Taking selfies to send to our other teammates that still weren't in Florida didn't help to use up my energy. Instead, it almost made it worse. And all of that energy just about tripled when we made it to the hotel.

"We're rooming together? Seriously?" Halley asked, jumping up and down in the lobby of the hotel.

"As long as you behave," her mom told her, although she was smiling as she said it. "And our room is right next door, so if you girls are up acting crazy too late, we will know. Not to mention there's a door that connects the rooms together that will stay open basically all the time."

While they went over rules with us for a few more minutes on the elevator ride up to our floor, we did our best to listen. Apparently, Halley and Lexi's moms were going to stay in one room together, and then Halley's dad and my dad were staying in another room together. Since Lexi's dad wasn't coming until later in the week, the moms decided they wanted to have their own 'girl time' like we would get. It was fine by me, since it meant we were finally all together in one room, unlike other competitions where only two of us were in one room at the most. Lexi's mom had already been staying at the hotel for the week since she was in town to watch Michael compete at Worlds, so Halley's parents and my dad went over the rules, again and again, to make up for one less parent being present in the elevator.

Finally, after the full lecture on the way up, we were given the keys to our hotel room. As soon as we opened the door, the excitement somehow reached an even higher level, something I didn't think was possible by that point. The room had a small kitchenette near the door, complete with a mini fridge and microwave. There was also a table and four chairs, perfect for breakfasts before heading to practice or the park. We all took in a rather standard set of two queen size beds, a small couch, a large dresser, a TV mounted on the wall, and lots of storage space in the closet near the bathroom. It was similar to other hotels we had been in for competitions and had nothing to do with the jumping and screaming that began as soon as the door was open and we stepped into the air conditioned room. That reaction was caused by the treats waiting for us.

Sitting on the small table right in front of us was a basket filled with TNT Force gear and other gifts. I knew it was likely part of the surprise my dad was so happy about, something he likely also had a hand in planning. There were power bars, protein shakes, Gatorade, and a variety of junk food. All of which were mostly red, with a few purple ones here and there so both Blast and Fuze were represented. As if that was not exciting enough, there were black drawstring bags with the TNT Force logo in gray and silver glitter.

Above the logo, each bag had one of our names on it, embroidered in red thread.

"We got new shirts!" Lexi announced as she opened her bag and started pulling out items. "And tank tops!"

As I opened my bag I saw she was right. In each bag was a black tank top similar to the one we wore to the gym every day. But instead of the usual gym logo, it was decorated with silver and red rhinestones on it that said '2016 Summit.' The zero was made of a Minnie Mouse head complete with a red bow. The shirt included in the bag was a red basic short sleeve shirt with the TNT logo in sparkly silvers and blacks on the front, and SUMMIT CREW on the back. Unlike Halley and Lexi, my bag held the same two clothing items again, only with purple as the main color to represent Fuze. Finally, we each got new bows, mine in both red and purple. They were a super flashing tick-tock bow with a shiny black on one side, and either shiny purple or red on the other half. On the team-colored side there was also a silver glitter outline of Cinderella's castle on the tail of the bow, and the TNT Force gym logo on the top loop. They matched the new tank tops perfectly and were likely the bows we would wear when we competed.

"So what do you think?" Halley's mom asked from the doorway where she and the other parents stood taking photos and videos of us opening our surprises.

"This is awesome" Lexi announced while I added, "So much glitter."

We all began laughing but were cut off when my cell phone sounded an alarm. Moving into action, my dad pulled his laptop out of his bag and handed it to me. I had it booted up in seconds and pulled up the familiar Worlds live feed immediately. Then, holding our breaths with anticipation, we all gathered around the screen to watch Nitro compete in the world finals.

CHAPTER 25

Watching Nitro was not the fun experience I assumed it was going to be. After seeing them almost hit on day one, then perform a flawless routine on day two I was certain they were easily going to grab a top spot in their division. I held my breath as Paul lifted Emily into the air, praying the stunt wouldn't be bobbled like on day one. Thankfully it stayed in the air, and the routine kept going. Sadly, after the partner stunt was over and the tumbling passes were finished, the routine began to fall apart. Literally.

The entire right side of the pyramid fell, not even getting through the first move before it crumbled. The five fliers that were in the pyramid went up for a heel stretch that would then start the sequence for the rest of that part of the routine, but something went wrong. Leanne, who always stayed in the air for every competition, lost her balance and starting falling to her left. The bases under her couldn't correct it, so as she went down she fell on top of the next stunt team over. That was when Victoria also went down, and it looked like she kicked someone in the face pretty hard on her way to the blue mat. The other side of the pyramid kept going in hopes of getting some points, but it wouldn't even begin to make up for the deductions caused by the stunt falls. The whole team seemed so confused and out of synch by the dance portion, there was no energy in their performance. When the music ended everyone just walked off the mat looking extremely dejected.

Lexi was on her phone right away, calling her mom who was in the arena to see the performance live. I stared at my phone then, not sure what to do. At the thought of texting Connor, I realized I didn't know what to say. Although he had been there for me time and time again when Blast didn't come in first, in that moment I didn't know the right words to express my feelings at all. It was partly because watching their performance had me thinking about more than just how Connor felt.

I was thinking how I would feel if I was in his place on the Worlds stage. And also how upset I would be if that was me in just a few days on one or both of my Summit teams.

I conveniently put my phone on silent and left it on the table with our new gear while I got ready for dinner. We were planning to spend a little time getting unpacked before we went to the pizza party for everyone who was already in Florida for Summit, as well as everyone who had just competed in Worlds. It was during that time we got the news that Bomb Squad came in third in their division and that despite a flawless routine Detonators ended up in fourth. Halley commented that the divisions were all full of great teams so the Worlds title was anyone's for the taking. Well, anyone that hit their routine. That was not the case for Nitro. I thought this, but of course didn't say anything out loud.

Once it was finally time to head to the pizza party I was getting more and more nervous about seeing Connor and what I could say to him to make him feel better. The truth was, I wasn't good at things like that. I always wanted to win and hated when people tried to act like it was okay when I didn't end up on top. So, when it came to encouraging other people for being less than the best, I didn't know what to do. In fact, I was so distracted by it all, I walked out of our hotel room without my phone.

"Let's take a selfie!" Lexie announced as we rode the elevator down to the party. "Let me use your phone, Max, it has the best camera."

"I don't have it," I told her after patting the pockets of my jean shorts. "I think I left it in the room."

"Should we go back?" Halley asked, reaching out to stop the elevator before it could reach the ground floor.

"No," I said with a quick shake of my head. "Anyone I want to talk to is going to be at the party."

My friends didn't push the issue but instead stood on either side of me for a photo. They were both wearing their new black Summit tank tops with the shiny red stones. At their insistence, I was wearing the same tank top, but in purple. I tried to tell them we should all match, but they reminded me it would match my makeup. Not only that, it would also make for cool photos with me in the center in my different shirt and them on either side of me. Part of me thought it was a little odd, but I was used to weird ideas like that from them by that point of our friendship for sure.

"Should I post it to Snapchat?" Halley asked after taking the photo.

"No way," Lexi told her before I could answer. "We can't ruin the hair surprise now. Not when we're so close to Connor finally seeing Max."

"You two are crazy," I stated simply, just as the elevator door opened.

We walked through the hotel lobby, outside the hotel, and then over to the picnic table area where balloons and banners announced the TNT Force Gym party. As we walked closer and closer to the party area, we were greeted by other athletes, giving them hugs and congratulations for a job well done at Worlds. I even heard Halley and Lexi compliment people from Nitro, despite their less than great final performance. As they did this, I tried my best to put on a smile and go along with it. I also said a "good job" here and there, but while I did that I was scanning the crowd. I knew Connor was somewhere, and as my best friend at the gym other than Halley and Lexi, I knew seeing him was the moment that mattered. I only hoped that when I did see him I would finally know what to say.

"There he is," Lexi said in my ear as if she knew what I had been thinking.

I turned to where she was looking, and spotted Connor walking towards the three of us. But, when I made eye contact with him and attempted to smile, he froze. Glancing at Halley and Lexi I was certain they were waving or making a face or something. But they weren't looking at me or Connor at all. They were talking to a girl on Bomb Squad I didn't know. Realizing that, I was instantly confused. Why did he just stop? I lifted up my hand and gave what instantly felt like a super awkward wave. Thankfully it got him moving again. As he got closer and closer I still didn't know what to say, but I found myself actually smiling, excited to finally see him.

"Hey," he said, stopping a few feet from me. It was odd, but in that moment I was a little hurt he didn't hug me right away. "Max, you look...just...wow."

"Uh, thanks," I replied with a nervous laugh. "It's good to see you."

Instead of waiting for him to act first, I stepped closer to Connor and gave him a hug. I had hugged him many times by that point, but rarely, if ever, was I the one who initiated them. The fact that I did in that moment clearly confused him for a second or two. He froze, then finally hugged me back. The hug lingered a lot longer than usual, Connor's arms still wrapped tightly around me. When I finally stepped back he was giving me a look that I had recently seen a lot of from Peter. Unlike Peter, however, he seemed to shake it off pretty quickly.

"Your hair looks great," Connor said, actually reaching up to tuck a strand of hair behind my ear. The action was odd, but it happened so quickly I didn't really respond. "I'm glad you're finally here."

"Me too," I said easily. "Your stunts looked great all weekend."

The compliment was the best I could manage off the top of my head. I figured it was okay to mention his stunts in particular, since he wasn't on the side of the pyramid that went down, and he also didn't have any bobbles or falls in any of his partner stunts or baskets. Sure, his team as a whole didn't do their best, but I felt like bringing that up would be rubbing salt into the wound. Sitting through awards was likely not an easy time for him and the others on Nitro.

"Thanks, Max," he said. "Only 363 days until Worlds next year. Lots of time for improvement."

I was a little shocked at his optimism, but I couldn't help but smile along with him in that moment as well. I didn't know if I would have felt the same way in his shoes. And I was hoping I wouldn't get to find out before Summit was over. But, for the time being, it was kind of nice to make light of what I'm sure was a hard blow for him and his team.

"Okay, we need pizza," Halley said to me, startling me for a second. I had been so focused on Connor I almost forget her and Lexi were standing next to me. "You guys coming?"

"Yeah," I nodded, my stomach growing at the thought of food.

"Right behind you," Connor added. Then, as if to make up for not hugging me first, he wrapped an arm around my shoulders and walked with me as we headed to a picnic table covered in pizza and other assorted treats.

CHAPTER 26

Monday night proved to be the kick off to Summit we all needed. Having time to hang out with all the Worlds athletes was so much fun. The fact that Leanne didn't stay for much of the volleyball and bonfire time was an added bonus! Feeling her glare on me all night would have made it a lot less fun for sure. But, at the same time, I felt a little bad knowing part of the reason she left the party early was due to the emotions of dropping her stunts. If I were in her shoes, I wouldn't have wanted to stay and hang out with everyone all night either. And realizing that I for once had sympathy for Leanne was a bit of a shock, to say the least.

Tuesday morning was a little sad when we had to say goodbye to Connor and the other athletes that were heading home. We headed to Downtown Disney afterward, so that helped us not think about it too much. A few of the athletes from Worlds were staying for Summit, but they enjoyed a nice sleep in before joining us at the parks. Matthew, Lexi's brother, as well as Gwen, were just some of the athletes that stayed. I didn't think much about it ahead of time, but it was a lot of fun to hang out with everyone outside of the gym and just enjoy Disney!

While we were in the park we spotted a lot of other people wearing cheer bows and their gym clothing. I noticed them all in passing, but my entire focus was the rides. We rode every ride we could, getting fast passes as often as possible so we could really take advantage of getting to Florida a day early. The constant rushing to the next ride was fun, but also made it an exhausting day. When we finally made it to the hotel that night, I went right to bed, knowing there was going to be a lot of practice once I woke up. After all, I was practicing with two teams and knew it would be extra hard work running full outs in the Florida heat.

As expected, Wednesday and Thursday were all about practice. Sure, we got to go to the parks for part of the day. But, that wasn't until after we made it through hours of hard work. And, also as expected, my friends were all dismissed well before me to go get showered and changed for the day each time. Halley and Lexi offered to wait for me, but I always told them to go ahead. It was easy enough to find them once I was done sweating and flipping and flying with Fuze.

"You can skip this full out," Nicole told me Thursday morning as we were setting up for yet another run through with Fuze. "I don't want you to get overheated."

"I'll be okay," I said with a shrug, then moved to get set up to run the routine once again.

It was hot out, to say the least, but I knew that running the routine was going to keep me from making any sort of mistakes. Not only that, but it also didn't seem fair for me to get to skip a run through just because I had already been practicing for a while with Blast. If no one else on Fuze got to skip the run through, then I needed to also work hard and push through, no matter how hot it got. Hot actually might have been an understatement. We were practicing outside during Summit, so if felt like I was a lobster baking in the sunshine while also getting overheated from running the routines.

"Great job ladies," Nicole said as we all gathered around after we were finally done practicing. "Everyone but Max needs to be out here tomorrow morning for our final team practice before we begin performance Friday. It's just for an hour, and then everyone will be heading over to watch and cheer on Blast. You don't need to do full hair and makeup when we go to watch them, but everyone needs to wear a gym shirt and bow. Remember you are always representing TNT this week, even if you're not up there on the stage. Now go have some fun, and remember to wear lots of sunscreen. Cheering this weekend is going to be no fun if you have a sunburn."

With that, we were all dismissed to have the rest of the day to ourselves. The extra practice had me super hungry, and food was all I could think about as I walked towards my room to shower. So, when my dad asked me if I wanted to get lunch with him before heading off to find Lexi and Halley, I agreed easily. After I took a nice long shower to wash off all the sweat from practice, my dad and I found a seafood restaurant near our hotel. I was excited to eat, and it was basically all I could think about. But, once we got our meals and started eating, I was shocked at the conversation my dad started.

"I sent an e-mail to Coach Varlee last night," he said between bites of his lunch.

"Really?" I asked, having almost completely forgotten about the softball clinic. Being nonstop busy with cheer practice and having fun in the park left me with no time to think about softball or anything relating to it.

"I figured we should let him know why you missed the clinic," he explained. "It would be one thing if you were just being lazy or weren't interested. But to miss it for being dedicated to not just one but two all star cheer teams is different."

"Wait, what?" I wasn't sure I knew what my dad was trying to say. After the way Cate and Ella and the other girls acted when they found out I was a cheerleader, I worried that telling Coach Varlee about it was a bad idea. Sure, the stunts after I got hurt helped with everything at least a little, but I was worried all the same.

"I just told him why you missed," my dad began again. "I let him know we were in Florida for Summit, and you couldn't leave later since you committed to the teams. I kind of figured that he didn't know what Summit was, so I also explained that a little."

"I don't think he cared much about cheerleading," I mumbled, already imagining

259

him laughing at me for missing softball for cheer.

"He was actually really impressed." My dad's words caught me off guard and had my full attention instantly. "His niece used to cheer at TNT Force, so he knows the type of dedication and talent it takes to do cheerleading. In fact, he wrote me back and told me that you being so involved with cheer was another point in your favor. He was kind of bummed you couldn't be there for the clinic to catch for his daughter, but said he was looking forward to seeing how you do at tryouts."

"He said that?" I asked him.

"Yes." My dad was trying to keep a straight face, but I could tell he was also extremely proud of me. "It doesn't mean you definitely have a spot on his team this year, but he has his eye on you. I think if he saw you catching with his daughter it would have sealed the deal, but you still have a good chance."

Nothing was certain yet, but the idea that I had a good coach keeping an eye on me at the upcoming tryouts was really cool. Well, it was mostly exciting, I should say. In that moment, something dawned on me that made my mood settle down a bit. Being on a top team like Varlee's Construction meant I would be extra busy with practice and even tournaments all spring and summer. Part of me had known that all along, but until it was so close to actually happening it was like I had been ignoring the commitment time.

I knew if I made that good of a softball team it would mean I would be doing a lot of extra practices and have next to no time with my friends all summer. And not just my friends. I would possibly also have to miss things like cheerleading conditioning, open gyms, and even my stunt class. So, as I sat there thinking it over, for the first time I was actually thinking about whether or not I even wanted to do softball. The thought was insane, especially after missing the basketball season already for cheer. I attributed my line of thinking to too much time in the sun. I assumed I was merely just caught up in the fun of Summit and not thinking clearly.

"Do you think the gym will mind if I have to miss things for softball all summer?" I asked, not totally able to drop the idea of juggling two sports.

"We can talk to your cheer coach and see what they think when the time comes," he suggested.

"I don't think Nicole will be too happy about that," I mumbled, trying to imagine how she would react to a summer schedule involving a lot of missed cheer practices for softball.

"Nicole might not be your coach next year," my dad pointed out, stopping me dead in my tracks yet again.

"Why wouldn't she be?" I asked him, genuinely confused.

"Your skills aren't just level 3 or even level 4 anymore sweetie," he explained. "Not to be a part of all the gossip or anything, but a few parents told me they heard the coaches mention the idea of putting you on Nitro or Detonators next year."

"But those are level 5 teams," I reminded him.

"Exactly," he nodded. "You have your full, and can do all the flying easily. Nitro has three athletes aging out this year, and a few more might be leaving for Detonators or Bomb Squad. That means they will be looking for some new talent to add to the team, and your name has been coming up. And if you can't stunt with the guys there, then you could easily get a position on Detonators. I think I heard at least seven people age out this year, including their center flier."

I started at my dad, not sure what I was more shocked about. On one hand, hearing my dad dish out all the inside info from the parents at TNT was strange. But, on the other hand, the idea that people really thought I could move up to level 5 team was a bit much to take in. I had all of the skills and everything, but moving up to Nitro or Detonators would mean a lot of changes. Not only would I possibly be on the same team as Connor, I would be going up against some really hard teams. And I would also have a shot at going to Worlds. It wasn't like anything was written in stone, but even the idea of it was a lot to take in.

"If I really did make it onto a level 5 team do you think missing practice for softball would be okay still?" I ask my dad, despite knowing it was information he likely didn't have.

"I guess that's something you will have to deal with when the time comes," he finally said.

And it was true. There were so many things that I would have to think about and deal with once Summit was over. Getting onto a good softball team was important. But so was cheer. For a lot of different reasons. It was a lot to try to think about and take in, especially after choosing Summit over the pitching clinics already. Instead of stressing too long about it, I pushed all of those thoughts aside so I could focus on simply making it through the next few days. It didn't matter what would happen come summer. What mattered was that I had to compete and do my best all weekend in Florida. Then, when it was all over, I could try to make a decision one way or the other. Hopefully.

CHAPTER 27

"Straight leg and you got this," Halley said to me just before I was tossed into the air for my full around.

"Awesome Max," Anna said as I landed, then moved into the next move.

Their familiar words of encouragement helped me focus as we ran the routine backstage at Summit. We were just minutes from taking the stage, and for the first time in a long time I was feeling nervous about hitting the blue mat in front of the crowd. It was weird, but knowing that it could be the last time I performed with Blast was suddenly nerve-wracking. Thankfully, everything was hitting in our run throughs. That fact was helping me keep the nervous edge off. More or less.

"Gather up ladies," Nicole called to us as we finished our last run through. We all walked closer to her and linked arms as we made a group circle, a pre-performance ritual. "When you get out there I want you to be confident and have fun. You have worked hard these last few weeks, and I know you can do this. Take a deep breath, remember what we're fighting for, and just hit everything one skill at a time. This could be the last time we perform this routine. Or, we can leave it all on the mat and prove to those judges we should be on that stage again tomorrow. Now hands in!"

We all put our hands into the center and began the cheer that we called out before every competition of the whole season. "TNT, TNT, TNT, BLAST!" After bobbing our hands up and down each time we called out TNT, we threw our hands up into the air on BLAST and stepped away from the center. Then, as always, we hugged someone close to us and began the walk to the stage. As we moved I found Lexi and Halley, holding their hands and giving their fingers a squeeze. Every competition started like that, the three of us linked together. Finally, with a deep breath and a big smile, I walked onto the mat with them once again. I spotted my dad in front of the stage with the other TNT parents and dropped my friend's hands to give him a two hand wave. Once he returned the wave I walked to my spot on the mat and waited for the music to start.

The next 2 and a half minutes were a blur. I was in the air, tumbling across the mat, and basically just doing my best to hit everything. Around me, I could see the girls on my squad also putting everything they had into the performance. When we reached the final pose at the end of the routine the crowd was screaming so loud I knew it meant only one thing: we hit! We hit every stunt, tumbling pass, and dance move in the routine. I wasn't sure in that moment if it would be enough to make it onto the next day of competition, but it felt good to know we had done everything we could and it was now all up to the score sheets.

"That was amazing," Lexi said, giving me a hug after we were backstage. "I think that's the best we've ever done!"

"Totally!" I agreed, turning away from her to hug more of the girls around me.

Everyone had so much energy after how well the routine went, and the excitement and celebration only began again when we were greeted by our family and coach. There were hugs and even happy tears from some parents as we all made our way towards the viewing booth to watch the playback of the routine. When we were finally done seeing the perfect routine on the playback screen the energy was almost too much to handle. In that moment I felt like I needed to go run around just to be able to function without exploding.

"Get a drink or something to eat then hang out close by," Nicole told us all, a massive smile on her face. "They will announce in just a little bit if we get to go on to tomorrow."

"I'm so nervous," Halley said to me, actually jumping up and down on the spot. "What if we don't make it?"

"We did our best, right?" I asked her, although I wasn't really expecting her to answer. "As long as we did what we went onto that mat to do, then we're golden. Even if the judges didn't like our dance or pyramid or anything, we have points from all the skills to get us into tomorrow. And then tomorrow we just have to hit again to move through to Sunday."

"And that is why you're my best friend," Halley laughed. "Just keep reminding me of that if I get any crazier."

"Will do," I promised her.

Walking over to my dad I took my red glitter cheer bag from him and pulled out my phone. I had one missed text along with a few snapchats and other notifications. Opening the text, I was happy to see it was from Connor.

"Great job Max. You ladies looked amazing out there. I would be shocked if you don't make it to day 2!"

It took me a second to realize that Connor had clearly been watching live online, the way I had watched him at Worlds. Based on the time difference back home he must have been in school, which was a little confusing. Did he go to the bathroom to watch? Was it between classes at the moment? Either way, I was so happy to have his support. Even if he wasn't there in person, knowing he was still thinking about me and following along felt great.

I replied to his text, then began a conversation about our division. Connor had watched all of the other teams we were up against, so he was letting me know how things were going in the division as a whole. Apparently, a few of the other teams had some stunt bobbles or tumbling falls, so that made me feel even more excited for awards. In fact, spending some time talking to Connor and relaying all of his messages to my friends made the time pass quickly. Before long we were ushered on stage to sit and wait to find out if we made it through to the next round.

"I feel like I'm going to die," Lexi said with a nervous laugh. She was sitting on one side of me, holding my hand in a death grip. Halley was on the other side of Lexi, and based on the look on her face she was also dealing with some painful hand holding.

"Well, if you don't, my hand might," I said to her, causing her to loosen her grip immediately. It only lasted a few seconds, but I found that squeezing her hand in return made it a little better.

Onstage, they were announcing the names of the teams making it into the semi-final round. I knew I would be performing the next day no matter what, but I wanted to be able to perform two times. Once with Fuze, and once with Blast. The longer the list of people making it through went on, the more the suspense was building. And, as the suspense was getting more intense, so did the vice grip Lexi had on my fingers. Before I could remind her to stop, the woman on the stage reached the end of her list.

"And the final team making it through to tomorrow's semi-final round is TNT Force Blast from Wichita Falls, Texas!"

I jumped up and started yelling and hugging my friends so fast I didn't even realize that it was happening. I felt like I was going to fall over from the sudden head rush of jumping up, cheering, and also screaming but managed to stay standing somehow. Part of it could have been the other girls on the team who were all crowded around me as they also hugged anyone they could reach. The chance to move on and really compete was the first step in getting to the finals, and it felt great to have the opportunity.

I could feel my phone buzz from where it was tucked into my cheer skirt. But, in that moment all I cared about was my team. I would have time later to send a text back to Connor, who was likely the one who texted me. In that moment the only thing that was important for me to focus on was the girls around me. Thanks to the 29 other members of Blast, we had another chance to prove we deserved a top spot in our division. And sure, we had another performance to make it through before we would find out if we made it to finals, but I was suddenly so confident in my team. It felt like we were reaching our peak at just the right time, and it felt amazing.

CHAPTER 28

"Does this look weird?" I asked Lexi as I got ready Saturday morning.

"Add a little more red to your left eye," she told me, then walked back into the bathroom to finish curling her hair.

I sat on the floor of our hotel room in front of the full-length mirror mounted on the wall. My makeup was spread out around me, and despite the practice runs I had done at home, I was trying a brand new makeup plan for the day. After I had done my hair and put in my red cheer bow, I applied my silver eyeshadow like always. Then, instead of layering on red glitter to go with Blast since I was performing with them first, I applied a mixture of purple and red glitter. This way, I figured, I wouldn't need to take off my makeup and put it back on before I performed with Fuze. Instead, I would just need to change my uniform and bow. It was still going to be a lot, but I was too excited for the whole day to worry about little things like changing between routines.

"We have to leave in 20 minutes," Lexi's mom announced through the open door that connected our room to theirs.

"Got it," Halley said as she walked out of the bathroom all ready to go. "Do you need me to do your eyeliner?"

"Yes please!" I grinned at her through the mirror. "I just need to do my bronzer first."

Brushing on the bronzer how I had been taught to apply it by my friends months ago, I looked at myself critically in the mirror before adding a little more blush.

"So are you ready to perform twice today?" Halley asked as she sat down next to me. I turned her way and she began applying the thick sweep of eyeliner.

"I think so," I replied, trying by best not to move while she worked. "It's kind of weird that the first time I even get to perform with Fuze is super important. No pressure or whatever."

"You know it's no pressure for you," Lexi interjected from her spot in front of the bathroom mirror. "You've hit everything in their routine from the first practice on."

"It took me a few days to get the dance," I said, trying not to move as I stifled a smile.

"But you stay in the air all the time," Halley finally said. "You don't need to stress. I mean, even if you did drop a stunt or miss a tumbling pass, the pressure isn't as big. You being on the team is helping them and making up for Cassidy being gone, so they will be happy you're there at all."

"No," I said actually pulling back from Halley. She was thankfully not applying eyeliner at the time, but still gave me a bit of a scowl. "If I drop something then I wreck what they have been working on all year. They've had a great season, and if I ruin it for them, it's all my fault."

"You're not going to ruin it for them," Halley assured me, her annoyed face totally gone. "You're going to go out there and hit your routines and be awesome. It's what you do Max. You may still need help with things like eyeliner, but you are a cheerleader through and through. When you hit that mat today, you're going to kill it. You're going to kill it for Blast and you're going to kill it for Fuze!"

I didn't know what to say in response. I more or less just nodded, smiled and then let Halley go back to finishing my eyeliner. Her comment was just about the nicest thing anyone could have said to me at that moment. Mostly because it was true. I cared about cheerleading and wanted to give it 100% all of the time. But thinking that way made me also think back to softball. Could I ever feel as good about any sport as I did about cheerleading? The idea was a strange one to have popped up like that, and I did my best to keep it out of my mind. After all, I had a lot of other important things to focus on. Like getting to the arena and performing not once but twice.

"Your makeup looks perfect," Lexi said to me as she finally came out of the bathroom followed by a cloud of hairspray. "The glitter looks really good."

"Thanks," I grinned as I stood up and grabbed my cheer bag. I checked it once more to make sure I had not only my usual backpack items but also my second uniform and bow. Once I knew I had everything I needed, I slipped it on and turned to my friends who were also dressed in their matching uniforms. "Ready to go?"

"Yup. Let's do this!" Halley replied, her face both determined and excited at once.

That was just what we did in fact. After making it to the area in time for some stretching in the hallway, we headed into the warm up room and were the same team from the day before. We were landing stunts and tumbling every run through, and the energy was building and building. But, as we walked onto the stage, the energy was starting to run dry. The routine we had been landing perfectly in warmups without even thinking about it was suddenly harder than ever. We were keeping everything in the air, but the energy on the mat was strange, to say the least.

"Straight leg and you got this," Halley said in my ear, and I found myself glancing at her in that moment before being tossed up for my kick single. She had a strained look on her face that almost made me forget to lock my body while in the air. As it was, I landed a little odd, but thankfully was caught and lowered to the mat like every other time we did the stunt.

When the dance portion of the routine came the energy picked up a little. This was likely because we knew we hit every element and skill we planned, and we also knew the routine was almost over. Being on the stage was somehow super stressful though, and until we hit the final pose it seemed like everyone in the audience was holding their breath and just waiting for everything to fall apart.

"We did it," Anna said giving me a smile as we walked off the mat. "Somehow we did it."

"We hit, right?" I asked her and the other athletes around me.

"I think so," Halley shrugged. "But I feel like we were trying to move through glue that whole time."

"Yeah," I nodded. "Everything felt really nerve-wracking out there."

Girls around me nodded as we walked around to where our families and friends were waiting for us. They gave us hugs and assured us we did great, but we all knew the truth. Just doing the skills and moves on the mats wasn't good enough. You needed to sell the routine and show everyone you were having a great time; something we failed to do during our performance. Watching the playback of the routine a few minutes later was almost painful in fact. There was just something lacking on the mat. Or maybe it was that something was there. And that something was nerves.

"It could have been a lot worse," Nicole assured us as we gathered up after we were done watching the playback. "If we make it to tomorrow we need to put our hearts into the whole routine. I know you can breathe life into everything, we just need to pray we get through to the finals and get that chance. You are all dismissed until Fuze performs in about an hour. Max," she said as she and the other 29 girls on my squad all turned to look at me. "You need to change and get ready for warm-ups. Fuze heads backstage soon."

The reminder was a bit shocking in that moment. I was still trying to wrap my head around what had just happened during Blast's performance, and now I needed to get backstage and ready to take the mat for a second time. With everyone watching me, looking so proud and excited for me, I felt about as nervous as I did while we were onstage moments before. But I didn't have time to focus on that. Instead, I just gave Nicole a nod and smile, then went to find my dad.

"You're going to be amazing sweetie," my dad told me as he handed me my cheer bag so I could go get changed.

"I hope so," I said in reply, not feeling as confident after the lackluster Blast performance.

"You don't need to hope," he said pulling me in for a big hug. "Just remember to take a breath and go out there and have fun."

"I'll try," I assured him, noting that I was hearing that same advice a lot lately.

"Now go get changed," he finally added. "Time to get purple."

With a laugh, I turned and headed towards the nearest bathroom. As I walked into the white tiled room, I wondered how many other athletes at the competition were changing clothing and performing for two teams. Were there a lot of us? Or was I the only one going back onstage just after getting off of it? There was no way to be sure. But, as I stepped into a stall and began changing I did my best to do what my dad said and just breathe. If I could put the performance I had just finished out of my mind and focus on what was next, then hopefully I could bring the energy to the Fuze performance that was missing for Blast.

CHAPTER 29

To a lot of people, it might seem like there is not much of a difference between one cheer team and another. For me, in fact, it took a long time to understand that different team levels meant different stunts and tumbling. For instance, I was only allowed to do a back tuck with Blast since it's a level three team. But, since Fuze is a level four team, I can throw layouts and whips while tumbling. And, if I were to move up to Nitro or any other level five team, I could end tumbling with a full. The rules for flying and basket tosses are even more detailed and confusing, so I mostly rely on my coaches to let me know what I can actually perform. Not to mention, on top of all of that, divisions have age restrictions as well. I may have been an 'older girl' on Blast, but I was the second youngest on Fuze.

All of these things can make a huge difference for a team. And all of that was evident the second I began warming up with the purple team backstage. Just an hour and a half before entering the warm-up room in my Fuze uniform and bow, I had been in there with Blast. With Blast, we would encourage one another to try hard while getting ready to perform, but we would also still laugh and play around. It was like we weren't taking things super seriously. Don't get me wrong, we still worked hard warming up the routine. But it was still more of a fun atmosphere than anything else.

The second we began warm-ups with Fuze I realized it was time to be serious through and through. Girls around me didn't joke around or act silly between stretches, and they never made funny faces at one another while waiting to take their turn warming up their tumbling. I didn't know if it was because people were older and somehow more 'mature,' but either way, it took me a second to hop on board. At first, I found myself feeling like I was going to scream if someone didn't do something silly or crazy. But then, the fierce and extremely focused attitude caught on and I found myself getting pumped to go on stage in a whole new way. I was ready to go out and perform, but also show everyone watching that I was tough and so much more than just a girl in a skirt and a lot of glitter.

"This is what you have been working for all year," Nicole said to the team, her speech much different than what she said to Blast before performing. "You have the heart and the talent, now go out there and hit this routine like never before. I know each of you has what it takes to get to tomorrow, but you need to show them. Show every judge and person watching that even if today is just the semifinals, you're walking away with rings this weekend."

At the mention of the championship Summit rings, a lot of girls started cheering, clapping, and even jumping up and down on the spot. I found myself even more fueled with energy and excitement right along with them. The mood was electric, and the idea of going onstage and making a big statement with a perfect performance was all I could think about.

"Hands in," Nicole finally said with a grin.

I tried to follow along the cheer I had only done with the team a few times, but mostly let everyone else say the words for me. The cheer, however, did a perfect job to get everyone even more ready to perform. "You lit the Fuze it's time to blow, get on that mat and start the show. We're here to win! We cannot lose! Let's hear it now, on three a Fuze. ONE, TWO, THREE! FUZE!"

It may have only been the first time I was performing for a real crowd with Fuze, but once I stepped out onto the mat and began the routine, it felt like I had done it a million times. Every move, stunt, and motion was like second nature as I worked with my teammates to perform all of the elements I had known for just a few short weeks. The serious mood before taking the stage was apparently just what I needed to land everything, all with a less than serious smile on my face.

When the routine ended and we left the stage, the crowd sounded so much louder than they had for Blast's performance just before. Part of this could have been because the girls on Blast were all at the edge of the stage screaming extra loud for me. But, whatever the reason was, it felt amazing. When I finally left the stage and made it to where Lexi, Halley, and the other girls in red were waiting, they all but knocked me to the ground. Clearly, they were proud of what I had just accomplished with my second performance of the day.

"Your tumbling was amazing!" Lexi gushed as soon as she was done giving me a massive hug. "You guys are totally going to make it to the finals."

"Well, we find out soon enough," I replied, although I had a huge grin on my face.

"I'm not going to lie," Halley began as she walked with me towards the playback station. "Seeing you do so well with Fuze made me a little shocked you weren't on that squad sooner."

"Thanks," I said, knowing Halley meant it as an amazing compliment.

Now, I have to admit that what Halley said was true. I really did fit in great with the girls on Fuze. Unless you knew it and were looking for me, you would not have been able to tell that I was the new person on the team. But, even as I watched the playback and saw how great we all looked, I was happy to still be on Blast. Fuze was a hard team and pushed me in new ways, but Blast was special thanks to my friends. Friends, I realized, that would be there to support me no matter what team we were all cheering on. Even if we were on different teams that didn't even compete or practice at the same time, we were friends no matter what.

"That's the best we've ever done," someone said, although I couldn't tell who it was that spoke. I realized then that I had been so lost in my thoughts that I didn't even get to see the replay of our performance. But, based on how it felt out there and how everyone was still buzzing with energy, I knew it must have looked pretty good. And that was good enough for me!

As we all finally walked away from the viewing booth, I found my dad. He had been hanging back a little to make room for all the girls crowding around Fuze. For a second I thought he might be annoyed I didn't find him as soon as I left the stage. But, based on his greeting I knew nothing could have been further from the truth. Picking me up to spin me around in a full circle, my dad set me back on the ground then planted a kiss on my forehead. The look of pride on his face after seeing me perform with Fuze for the first time was enough to get me feeling instantly emotional. Thankfully I didn't have to worry too long about the possibility of tearing up or crying.

"This thing has been buzzing like crazy," my dad said, pulling my cell phone out of his pocket and handing it to me.

Looking at the screen I saw I had missed messages from both Connor and Peter. Since I didn't check my phone between my two performances I saw many of them were about Blast's performance, and then also about the performance I had just done onstage with Fuze. I scanned through them quickly, trying to take it all in. Peter had been following along on Twitter, while Connor and some other athletes from the gym were watching the live feeds. Despite the two different ways of following my time at Summit, they both said one thing in almost the exact same words: "You're totally going to finals with both teams!"

CHAPTER 30

Sitting in the hotel room that night I found myself packing my bags, at a loss for anything else to do. The day was exhausting, to say the least, and while I waited for our late night room service pizza to arrive it was the only useful action that came to mind.

"You're already packing?" Halley asked with a frown. She and Lexi were sitting on one of the beds sharing a bag of gummy worms.

"I need to do something," I said as I put the last of my clothing items back into my suitcase and turned to face my friends. "I just have way too much energy right now."

"Then stretch or something," Lexi shrugged, slurping a long gummy worm into her mouth. "You can't pack now when you still have another day of performing and a day in the parks to look forward to."

"Yeah, I guess," I said with the shrug.

Stepping away from my suitcase I did what Lexi said and pulled my leg up behind my body and held it in place with both arms for a skill known as a needle. The goal was to keep both legs straight while you still kept your body upright so your leg up in the air was all but flat against your back. It was easy enough for me to hold, although when I had a team of people holding me up in the air I tended to wiggle a little too much and fall out of the stunt or at least not keep it quite as straight. But, standing in the hotel room I focused on holding the stunt perfectly still until the sound of Lexi and Halley laughing was too much of a distraction.

"What?" I asked them, finally dropping my left leg to the ground.

"I was just kidding," Lexi laughed. "I think you proved today you've done more than enough stretching for a while."

Deciding to give up on the needle for a while, I walked across the room and hopped onto the bed where my friends were lounging. I stole a few gummy worms then rolled onto my back and stared at the ceiling. After a few seconds, I realized it was the longest I had just sat down and done nothing since finding out that not just one but both of my squads were going to finals. The news had me jumping and skipping around the entire evening, too excited to stay still. It was just too much good news to move on from so quickly. Blast was in fourth going into the final, probably due to the lack of performance in our routine. Fuze, however, was in second. The team in first was only above us by a tenth of a point, so we needed to hit the final performance and also hope the first place team had at least one bobble in order for us to take home the first place rings.

"So do you think you're going to be on Fuze next year?" Halley asked, finally breaking the silence that was filling the room.

"Me?" I asked, rolling over to watch her as she nodded while eating another candy. "Maybe. But my dad kind of mentioned that some of the other gym parents heard coaches talking about me being on Nitro or Detonators next year."

"What?" Lexi yelped, actually jumping up so she was standing on the bed. "Are you serious? That's so awesome!"

"It's not that big of a deal," I tried to say, but Halley was quick to correct me.

"It's a big big deal!" she explained. "Those are level 5 teams that get to go to Worlds! And if you're on the squad maybe you can be there for either teams' first win!"

"You mean we've never won first at Worlds?" I asked, thankful Lexi was finally sitting back down on the bed.

"Nope," Lexi said with the shake of her head. "Our level 5 teams have gotten so many seconds and thirds, people actually made jokes and memes and all kinds of stuff about it."

"A year or two ago there was an Instagram account all about things TNT Force gym athletes can't do," Halley added. "It was after the year all three teams took second at Worlds, and the whole page was about everyone being second best and this and that. People got really upset about it and the account got taken down for bullying or something."

"Okay," I said slowly. "So why does it matter if I'm on Nitro or Detonators?"

"You're tumbling," Lexi said instantly. After seeing the blank expression on my face she continued. "We can work on partner stunts and good pyramids and dances and all that, but we don't have power tumblers. We need people who can do a pass, then just throw a punch front and do another great pass again. I don't think we've had a tumbler like you at the gym since Greg aged out."

"So thanks to my tumbling I could help us get the raw score up?" I asked, trying to wrap my head around everything I had just heard.

"Exactly," Lexi grinned.

"And you're really good at flying, so who knows what else they could do," Halley chimed in. "I bet you could do a kick single kick single basket."

In response, I just nodded, then tried to follow along as Halley and Lexi began to brainstorm the other stunts and skills I could do that would add to the overall team score and potential. What they were saying made a little sense to me, though. I was good at tumbling, and the smallest flyer my age. Lexi was a little lighter than me, but she was still too young to be on a senior team. That meant that I was the easiest to throw in the air for baskets and other skills. It seemed like a trivial reason for me to get placed on a squad, and at the same time I wasn't officially on any team yet for the upcoming season.

Skill assessments and try-outs were a few weeks away, so I would need to wait until then to really figure out what team I would make. Not to mention that between now and then I might also be placed on a softball team that required my attention. Since I knew there wasn't anything I could one way or the other, I went back to snacking on the gummy worms.

Lexi and Halley went on talking about my cheer future for a while longer. They might have talked all night, but thankfully the room service showed up and was the perfect distraction. We ate every slice of the large pizza, happy for the extra food since after dinner we had done a lot of swimming. But then, well before the time we claimed we were going to stay up until, we went to bed. It wasn't early, but it wasn't exactly late either. We just figured it would be good to get a lot of sleep for the next day. After all, Sunday had the potential to be a very important day for all the athletes on both Blast and Fuze.

CHAPTER 31

As soon as I woke up on Sunday morning
I could tell that something was different. It was just like most competition days in general, but when you looked closer it was like something was a bit off. It started the second I got out of bed. We had been joking and kidding around all night up until bed, but as we got up and got ready to leave for the competition, all of the joking was gone. For a while, it seemed to help me focus on what was to come. But then, as we sat watching teams perform before we got ready to head to warm-ups, I started to feel more and more anxious. Being so serious and intense for so long was leaving me feeling like I was going to explode.

"Are you okay?" Halley asked me as we sat watching a junior level 3 team on stage.

"What?" I asked looking at her suddenly. "Me? Yeah, I'm fine."

"Yeah right," she laughed. "You look like you're going to scream. Or maybe the real problem is that you literally need to scream."

"Yes," I nodded. "Both of those."

"Well calm down," she said simply. "You have nothing to worry about."

"Nothing?" I asked in reply. "I'm on two teams. That means two chances to let everyone down when I mess up."

"No," Halley corrected me immediately. "You have two chances to prove to everyone why you're going to be on a level 5 team next year. Two chances for everyone in this arena to realize how good you are at cheerleading. You're going to get out there today and perform two perfect routines like always, and we all know it."

"Not like always. I messed up a dance move when we were at the competition in Vegas," I said, knowing instantly it was a weak attempt to show her she was wrong.

"As I was saying," she continued with a laugh, "You have nothing to worry about."

In fact, as if to prove how right she was, the team on stage dropped part of their pyramid. They were a team that was ahead of us going into the finals, and seeing them fall was weird. It didn't make me happy, but in a way it was a good thing. Seeing them make a mistake was like taking a weight off my shoulders. That mistake gave us an even bigger opportunity to beat them. The second I thought that, however, I realized that wishing for someone else to do bad wasn't how I wanted to win. So, instead, I decided to use my extra energy to cheer for every team that took the mat before us.

"They just hit," Lexi frowned at me after a level 3 team we were up against finished on stage a few minutes later.

"I know. Wasn't it awesome?" I asked with a nod of my head as I continued clapping.

"What if they beat us?" she asked me, clearly confused by my reaction to them doing so well.

"Well, I don't know if their raw score was big enough or not," I began. "But I would rather win against teams that hit and made it hard for us, then win because everyone else had mistakes."

"You never cease to amazing me," Lexi replied. But, from that moment on, I noticed that she also joined me in my cheering.

In fact, by the time we went back to warm up with Blast, I noticed that most of the girls around me in red TNT uniforms were cheering for the teams onstage as well. Even once I was backstage stretching and getting ready to warm up my tumbling I was enjoying watching the other teams around me. Spending my time encouraging other people, even if it was just by watching and appreciating what they were doing was making me excited to show them all what I could do. Not to show off or rub it in their face, but rather to join in on the performing fun. It reminded me of how I felt at open gym times, and before long I couldn't help but compliment the people around me.

"That was an awesome tumbling pass," I said to a boy who was also backstage. After watching him warming up a tumbling pass, I simply had to say something.

"Thanks," he said, turning to give me a smile.

I gave a little wave and walked away to warm up my skills as well, feeling somehow even more excited. The idea of being able to walk up to someone and say "good job" and things like that was really fun. I didn't usually talk to other teams at competitions, but in that moment I was excited to start letting people know when I enjoyed their hard work and skills. It was apparently appreciated since the boy I complimented came over to return the favor after I did my own tumbling pass.

"That was really good," he said to me, actually holding his hand out. "I'm Daniel."

"Max," I said shaking his hand. I noticed he was wearing a white and light blue uniform, but wasn't sure what gym he was from.

"Good luck out there," Daniel said, then turned to follow his team out onto the stage.

The interaction took seconds but made me feel really great all the same. Instead of worrying about whether or not the athletes in my divisions were going to beat my teams, I could just focus on doing my best and wishing the same for the people around me. Despite the high level of competition, I felt more at ease than at the far less important softball clinics where no one seemed to show support for one another. Realizing that, part of me wanted to tell even more athletes good job. But, I also knew I needed to focus on my own team. So, I decided to do what I could to encourage the girls around me wearing red as well.

I found myself calling out "great back tuck" and "that was perfect" and "your height on that was insane" to the girls around me basically nonstop. Anytime there was even the smallest compliment to give, I made sure to scream it out. I noticed other girls were doing it as well, really making sure to build one another up before our performance. For the first time all season, our talking felt more genuine than all of our mat talk. As a result, by the time we walked out onto the stage I felt like there wasn't anything we couldn't do.

Unlike a lot of the times I performed, I was aware of every move I made, every beat of the music, and every stunt that was lifted or tossed into the air. Nothing was passing me by in a blur like usual. Time seemed to travel in slow motion as I flipped and tumbled and spun my way around the mat, all fueled by the comments everyone was calling out to each other.

"Kill it one last time!" Halley cheered me on before my kick single. She didn't remind me to keep my leg straight that time, but I managed the move perfectly all the same.

"That was flawless," Anna said once I was safely back on the ground.

"You guys rock!" I said in reply, then continued on to the next move in the routine.

When we reached our final pose after the two and a half minutes on stage, the response from the crowd was louder than any competition all season. As I was jumping and skipping and hugging my team, it suddenly hit me. We did it. We performed our routine the best we ever had before, and it was on the day that mattered the most. Based on the way the girls around me were also cheering, smiling, and even crying I knew that they were realizing the same thing as well.

"I'm so proud of you honey," my dad announced the second I made my way to where he and the other parents were waiting. He once again picked me up and spun me around, clearly still pumped up from watching me perform.

"Thanks, Dad," I managed when he finally set me down.

"You need to go change," he said then, handing me my purple uniform.

"What? Now?" I asked, looking around me as if someone else was going to pop out and announce that it was a joke.

"Fuze went to warm-ups a few minutes ago."

Immediately, the excitement from performing with Blast turned into panic at getting changed and backstage once again. I said a quick goodbye to my friends, then all but sprinted to the bathroom to change. I found Fuze backstage just as they were about to start running skills and pyramid.

"Max," Nicole called out to me and motioned me over to her.

"Yeah?" I asked walking towards her while still fixing my crooked uniform sleeve.

"Breathe," she said simply. "Take a breath, and give yourself a minute. You were perfect out there with Blast, and you can do it again with Fuze. But you need to relax."

I nodded, then turned and walked towards stunt team. Before I reached them though, I made sure to do what Nicole said. I actually stopped, closed my eyes and took a big breath. I held it for a few second before slowly let it out. Surprisingly I felt a lot less stress instantly. Once I was in place, Nicole gave me a thumbs up before counting us into the stunts. I was still a little nervous about getting back on the stage so soon but tried my best to not let it affect my performance. After all, I was only two and a half minutes away from possibly winning it all.

CHAPTER 32

When Blast performed, my energy was over the top. I felt every move and motion and skill the entire way through. When I performed with Fuze just moments later, it was a completely different experience. I found myself not just doing the motions and being aware of my body, but actually trying as hard as I could to get height on my back handsprings, to keep my legs straight while flying, and to make every arm motion sharp and clean. I didn't just do things, I overdid things, making sure they were the best I could make them.

My two performances of the day were different in that way, but not in much else. We hit everything clean and perfect from start and finish. When we finally walked off stage we were met with cheering and screaming and lots of happy hugs, all congratulating us for a perfect routine. I knew there was a while until we would get the results and find out who won at the awards ceremonies, but after hitting two flawless routines I was feeling pretty great. I took some time to snack on some trail mix, and then sent out replies to all of the texts I got about my two performances. Finally, knowing we had a while to wait, I walked with Halley and Lexi to look at bows.

"If we buy a bow now is that like saying we won't win?" I asked, not sure on the rules of that particular tradition.

"No," Lexi said immediately. "Today we just get to buy bows to buy them. Even if we don't get first we did our absolute best. This bow is simply about filling my need for something new and sparkly."

"You mean like a first place Summit ring?" I offered, having a hard time not thinking about the awards I knew were approaching quickly.

"Well, hopefully I'll get that too," Lexi grinned. "But I also want a new cheer bow to wear to tryouts. Something that will make me really stand out."

"You're not wearing a TNT bow?" I asked her, idly looking around at a few bows on the table in front of us.

"No way," Lexi replied.

"Tryouts are one of the only times we don't have to wear team bows," Halley added. "Well, and open gyms, but most people still wear team bows to open gyms. So tryouts are the best time to show off the awesome bows you own."

As we looked through another table of bows I noticed a set of three with 'BEST FRIENDS FOREVER' split across them. It was the same kind we had purchased a few weeks prior, only in different colors. Seeing it made me think how much had changed since then. When I bought that bow I was feeling less and less like a part of something great. I was all but ready to quit cheer since my team wasn't doing well. Now, just a short time later I was on not one but two teams that were in the finals at Summit. It was a little crazy to think about for sure.

"How about this one?" Halley asked, holding up a bow with cheetah print in a few bright colors.

"It's very you," I nodded, knowing I would never choose the bow for myself.

"I really want to get a chevron patterned one," Lexi commented while looking at the bows on the table. "But in a color I don't have. I think I already have red, pink, gold, and black."

"And you need another one?" I challenged her with a bit of a laugh.

"Well yeah," she replied while still looking. "I just got a new green chevron tank so I kind of need a bow to match it."

With a shake of my head, I went back to looking at more bows. A lot of them featured bright colors and were covered in sparkles and glitter. Nothing was really catching my eye, though. Lexi and Halley were debating between two bows so I made my way to another table. The second I walked up to that vendor a bow caught my eye. It wasn't sparkly or shiny at all, but rather was a tick tock bow without a single rhinestone attached. One half of the bow had "CHEERLEADER" split between the top and bottom strip of ribbon. The words were white, printed on a dark blue fabric that made them really pop. On the other half of the bow were a mix of blues, purples, pinks, and blacks combined to form a beautiful scene of outer space. Picking up the bow I saw that it was actually a printed on image of galaxies and stars, although I couldn't identify any of them. As beautiful as the space scene had been from far away it was even more perfect up close. I only had to think about it for a second, then handed my money to the woman behind the table.

"What did you get?" Lexi asked walking towards me. She was carrying two bows, both different colors of a glittery chevron pattern. When I showed her my bow, however, her jaw all but dropped. "That's so cool!"

"Let me see." The words were barely out of Halley's mouth when she gasped at the bow I picked. "It's perfect."

"I really like it," I said with a big grin. "I figure if I walk away from here with a nice new ring to wear, people are going to start figuring out I'm a cheerleader. So, I might as well beat them to the punch and have a bow that says it too."

"You mean you would wear something like that around your softball team?" Lexi asked as we turned and started walking to look at other bow tables. She had a look on her face that made it clear she assumed the bow would be hung up in my closed along with the others I bought all season at competitions.

"Maybe," I shrugged.

"Even if you get on a really good team?" Halley asked, obviously doubting me as well.

"I don't know if there's even a chance for me to get on a really good team," I finally admitted. "I had to miss a softball clinic on Tuesday since I was already here for Summit."

"Really?" Halley asked in shock. "Why didn't you just come late?"

"I thought about," I said honestly. "But then I thought about letting down not just one, but two teams. Not to mention missing the time in the park and the fun on the flight, and seeing the Worlds teams, and just everything. So now I have to really impress the coaches at the normal tryouts if I want to make a decent team. But, I don't know."

"What do you mean, you don't know?" Lexi asked. We had stopped walking and were standing a few feet from any of the vendor tables.

"If what my dad said is true and I might be on Nitro or Detonators, then maybe I need to decide between cheer and softball," I finally explained. "Being on a top softball team and being on a top cheer team just sounds like a lot. But if I don't get on a good softball team then who knows what I'll do."

"Well, what if you don't get on a really good softball team?" Lexi tried again. "I mean, do you really have to win all the time for softball to be fun?"

I paused then and looked at my friends while thinking it over. The question was a simple one and was almost the same exact thing Peter had asked me about cheerleading not long ago. Cheer felt less fun when my team wasn't winning, but what kept me going through the season was really my coaches and friends. Especially my friends. Without Halley and Lexi there to help me and support me I would have quit cheer before I even got started. But, thinking about softball, I realized I didn't have a lot of friends there. The girls on my past teams didn't hang out with me and get to know me. They already had their friendships formed from past seasons. Aside from Hillary and maybe one or two other girls I was friends with on social media, I wasn't walking into a group of girls that I felt connected with. Sure, the new age division could mean new friends, but it could also mean more of the responses I got at the pitching clinic when Cate told everyone I was a cheerleader.

I think that was the moment, standing there with my friends, that it finally clicked in my head. As much as I loved softball, there weren't a lot of people that were making it more than just a lot of hard work and growing as an athlete. Sure, that stuff was fun and great and all. At cheer, however, I was getting pushed and worked hard and also had the benefit of being surrounded by people that were really my friends. Not only were Lexi and Halley always there for me, but I loved working with all the girls on Blast. Everyone on Fuze was really nice too, even after the short time I had spent getting to know them. Connor, Gwen, Michael, and Reid from my stunting class were super amazing, not to mention I loved spending time with Greg, Tonya, and Nicole. TNT Force was like a family for me, and as much as I didn't like losing competitions, it was still better than winning and not having people to really celebrate with.

"Kind of," I finally said in reply to Lexi's question. "I don't have people like you guys at softball to make it worth it even if the team isn't winning."

"You mean not winning like Blast was for part of the season?" Halley asked, raising one eyebrow at me.

"No, I didn't mean-" I started to say, only to be cut off by Halley.

"I'm kidding!" she laughed. "Although it was clear you were bummed for a while there.

"Yeah," Lexi added after seeing the shocked look on my face. "It's hard to do something new and be so good at it and not get to win all the time. I get it for sure. But I'm really glad you decided not to quit the team early or anything."

"I didn't know you guys could tell," I said with a frown. "I'm a little worried for next season though, to be honest. You two are the best thing about cheer, and the idea of not being on the same team is kind of weird. I don't know if I can make new friends like you guys to make up for any competition we don't win."

"Then just win all the time," Halley said with a smile. "Nitro or Detonators could really win it all if you're there to help. No joke."

"And we're still friends too, remember?" Lexi added with a grin. "I don't care what team you're on, or what classes you take. We're still going to be friends. We've been through too much this season to just move on like it was all no big deal."

I nodded, thinking immediately of the first time I really opened up to Lexi and Halley. They sat with me as I told Tonya that I didn't feel like I would ever fit in at the gym. I also told them that night that the reason I didn't like people calling me Maxine was because only my mom called me that, all the way up until she died. I actually cried that night, opening up to Tonya and my new friends, something I never did around anyone but my dad. Sure, I hadn't cried around them after that day, but it was something that made our friendship really strong. Being a tomboy, I never thought I would end up with friends like Lexi and Halley, but now that they were a part of my life I knew I wanted them there forever.

"You're right," I nodded. "We'll always be best friends. Even if I make other good friends on Fuze or Nitro or whatever. The gym is awesome like that. I can have lots of friends. But at softball, I think I would only ever have teammates."

"Wait, are you not even trying out then?" Lexi asked.

"I don't know," I shrugged. "For now, I'm just focusing on the rest of Summit."

"Speaking of which, I think awards are soon," Halley announced, checking the time on her phone. Sneaking a peek over her shoulder I saw we had just over 15 minutes.

"We should head back," I decided for us, turning to walk that way immediately.

Lexi and Halley fell into step on either side of me, linking their arms with mine. In only a few more minutes I would find out if Blast were the Summit champions we were all hoping to become. And then, not long after that, I would find out if Fuze landed in the top spot as well. It was going to be a long afternoon, but as we walked back to where the athletes and parents from TNT Force were waiting, all I could think about was how lucky I was.

Not just lucky that I was about to possibly win not one, but two Summit rings. And not just lucky that I was able to compete in a cool place like Disney World. In that moment I felt lucky that my friends were by my side, my dad was there to cheer me on, and I had even more friends cheering me on at home. I knew when I checked my phone it would show missed texts and snapchat messages from people letting me know they were excited and waiting for awards, just as much as I was. That was something no one ever did for me when I played any other sport or did any other kind of school activity. So, as we waited impatiently until we were invited to take the stage to find out the results for Blast, I couldn't wipe the smile off my face. Ring or no ring, in that moment, with people I cared about all around me, I felt like I had already won. And that feeling was better than any banner, medal, or ring any day.

ABOUT THE AUTHOR

Dana Burkey is a self-published author living in

 Washington State. Although she is from Ohio, she has been enjoying life in the Pacific Northwest for the last 7 years. Before moving to Washington, Burkey attended college in Ohio where she majored in theater with a minor in creative writing. Burkey works full time in camping, spending her days with K-5th graders. She began self-publishing her YA romance novels in August of 2014, hoping to write stories that can be enjoyed by YA readers of any age. Her books feature a lack of swearing, drinking, and sex, in an effort to allow younger readers to connect with her stories without bad influences. Burkey is currently working on a few projects, which she is looking forward to sharing with readers soon!

Rock your very own Best
Friends Forever cheer bows,
as seen on the back cover!
Order now from the Etsy shop
MySIXChicks to get this set, or
any of the other amazing bows
on sale now!

Get your very own Summit bows, as seen on the cover, from the Etsy shop CraftyOhBows!
Many options available, including custom orders!

SNEAK PEEK

Continue reading for a sneak peek at book 3 in the TNT Force Cheer series, Center Stage! For more information about this book and others, or to rate the book you just read, be sure to check out Dana on Goodreads or Amazon.

CHAPTER 1

"Alright Max, whenever you're ready."

I nodded at the assistant coach that had spoken, then stepped onto the blue spring loaded floor in front of me. Standing on the white line representing the edge of the performance space, I took a deep breath, closing my eyes as I let out a long exhale. I shook out my hands, mostly to get rid of the extra nervousness and jitters I was feeling. Then, I opened my eyes and focused them on the spot across the mat where I would land. Finally, I took off to perform the moves I had been working on for the last three weeks in the gym.

Once I had taken a few running steps forward I slammed my feet down at the same time and used the momentum to flip myself over in a front flip more commonly known as a punch front. As soon as my feet hit the ground I pushed off and performed a round off before flipping my body over once again in a back handspring. With the speed and height I had built up I was able to keep my body straight for two more flips. Since my body wasn't bent at the knee the flips were known as whips and gave me the power I needed for my final skill. Pushing with my legs as hard as I could, I performed another back flip, however this one included two twists of my body before I landed on my feet. Known as a double full, the move was the perfect difficult ending to my tumbling pass.

"Great job!" Someone called out, but I was too busy breathing a sigh of relief to figure out who it was. It didn't help that there were also a few people clapping and cheering for me from around the gym. Not wanting to stay in the spotlight too long, I stepped off the mat and allowed the next cheerleader to perform their tumbling pass.

"How did it look?" I asked my best friend as I walked towards her and took the water bottle she was handing me.

"Your height on the double full was the best I've ever seen it," Lexi said honestly. "I think you could have added a kick and still landed it. You should try it on your next pass."

"I don't know about that." I drank a little more water then wiped the sweat off my face. When I pulled my hand away and saw the smudge of eyeliner I turned to Lexi with a frustrated look. "This is why I said no makeup."

"Come on," she laughed, then grabbed my arm and pulled me a few feet away into the bathroom.

Walking to the mirror I was happy to see that I had only smudged the thin layer of black eyeliner a little, and thankfully didn't take off any of my light purple eyeshadow with it. I never wore makeup to practice at the TNT Force cheerleading gym, but Lexi insisted I needed to look good for skill evaluations. After using my finger tips to get the makeup back under control, I stepped towards the sink and wet a paper towel. My face was flushed after the two hours of working out. Although we had just begun the assessment time, like many athletes I arrived to the gym early to finish working on everything I would perform for the coaches and cameras watching.

I patted my face and neck with the wet paper towel, trying to cool off at least a little before walking back out into the gym. My skin was going to stay pink no matter what I did, but at least my hair was in place. This was due to the layers and layers of hairspray I put into my short brown hair while teasing and combing it into a half pony tail complete with a sparkling cheer bow. The bow was one I received once I returned home from Summit, a national cheerleading competition just a month before assessments. There were a few others in the gym that day wearing their custom championship bow, a rather simple bow with the summit logo mounted in the center. But, unlike the other bows, mine represented not just one but two first place wins. My bow had both red and purple glittery fabric surrounding the competitions logo. This was thanks to pulling double duty and performing with two TNT Force Cheer squads, something that was giving me lots of confident going into the new season. After all, I was the first athlete at the gym to walk away from Summit with two first place titles, not to mention I would be getting two championship rings to celebrate as well.

"We need to get back out there," Lexi reminded me, adjusting her red bow in the mirror. It was surrounded by her curled and styled white blond hair.

"I know," I said with a long sigh. "Ready or not, here we go."

"Come on," she laughed. "You are totally ready and you know it."

Shaking my head at her words I simply followed her out of the bathroom and back into the room filled with athletes working to showcase their skills and impress the gym staff. It was the second day of the assessments, the first having been spent learning dances and basic cheerleading choreography. I was happy to say all but a few dance moves were easy enough for me to learn. It was not nearly as bad as the first time I was tasked with dancing on one of the gyms blue mats with an audience watching. There were still a lot of people better than me at dancing, but that's why I was happy for the second day to show my stuff.

Parting ways with Lexi as she moved across the gym to show off her standing jumps, I once again lined up for the tumbling floor. The TNT Force gym was a long and tall industrial room with stark white walls, one of which was covered with mirrors. There were four blue mats making up the length of the room, all with spring loaded floors to help us jump and cheer our best. Between eight rows of mats were a set of cubbies for the athletes to store their gear. Closest to the door were the gym offices, as well as a parent viewing area that was usually filled with adults. During assessments, however, parents were forced to stay outside, and couldn't even peek in thanks to the paper covering the windows. At the far end of the room, farthest from the gym's main entrance, were a series of running tracks, trampolines, and foam pits, all for athletes to use while working on new skills. I had logged many hours over the weeks since Summit making sure I was ready to showcase all that I could do. Now, it was time to show every judge and member of the gym what I had learned.

"Alright Max, you're up," the same coach as before called to me. If I remembered correctly her name was Molly, but since she was a junior level 2 coach I hadn't spent any time with her since joining the gym.

Stepping onto the mat I looked over where Nicole stood on a larger scaffolding style platform set up for the assessments. As both a coach as well as one of the gym's owner, Nicole had coached both of my teams the year before. Around her on the platform were three cameras, used to catch everything occurring on the mats during the night. One pointed towards the stunting mats where girls were lifted and thrown into the air by skilled bases, another was aimed on the standing jump mat where athletes would perform toe touches and hurdlers and back tucks. The final camera was trained on the mat I was about to race across once again. It was my second and final tumbling pass of the afternoon, and I knew I needed to make it count. I realized Nicole was watching me just before I turned away from facing her, and it made me even more confident in what I was about to do. After all, Nicole pushed me to get better and better at cheerleading. And now I could land skills that truly were better than ever.

Taking off across the blue floor I once again began my pass with a punch front followed by a round off. Next, I wiped my body around while twisting, performing a full before my feet met the ground once again. The move slowed me down more than I wanted it to, but I had planned for that. I pushed as hard as I could and used the extra momentum of a back handspring to transition into a whip. That final move gave me the height I needed for the very thing Lexi had encouraged me to do. Kicking my leg up as high as I could, I reached for it with one hand then brought it back down as I immediately began corkscrewing my body, all while flipping through the air. The resulting kick double full was the hardest move I had been working on, and was one I hadn't officially mastered. But, I was determined to land it when it counted, with Nicole and so many others watching. As my feet hit the floor, however, I knew I didn't quite have the force needed. I found myself stepping first one, then another foot forward, then finally falling to my knees. Despite my best effort, I hadn't landed the skill as planned.

I quickly stood up, mad at myself for not sticking to the safer kick single I had been planning before Lexi's encouragements. I turned to walk off the mat, and only then realized people were cheering for me. Glancing towards where the noise was the loudest, I was happy to see that not only were my friends cheering, Nicole was also clapping enthusiastically from her perch with the cameras. Knowing I needed to leave the mat for the next athlete I quickened my pace to a jog, but couldn't help the massive grin growing on my face. Sure, I didn't land the kick double, but based on everyone's reaction they were proud of me. Likely because they knew I was on track to get it soon enough. And that meant that the chance of landing on a top team at the gym was getting more and more possible all the time.

CHAPTER 2

Despite the cheers from everyone in the gym I was still a little disappointed in myself for trying the kick double. It felt good that I was close to landing the hard move, and I knew I would be in the gym for hours and hours to perfect it. But first, I needed to finish the rest of my assessments. After getting some water and stretching for a few minutes I headed to the mat at the far end of the room where I would need to display my skills in the air.

"You ready to fly Max?" Lenny asked. When I nodded to let him know I was ready to fly, he gave me a quick fist bump then called over three athletes that would serve as my bases.

Lenny was a coach that had been gone for the previous competition season while at college. He was back for the summer, and the rumor around the gym was that he was going to be on staff full time for the upcoming cheer season. Although I had only met him twice before the assessments began, I already loved being around him. He was intimidating when you first met him thanks to his large frame and bulging muscles. He had thick dreadlocks to his shoulders and two arms covered with dozens of colorful tattoos that still showed up easily despite his dark skin. On top of that, his face seemed to be in a scowl when he was concentrating, only adding to his overall scary guy image. However, I quickly learned he was the funniest coach at the gym, and knew everything there was about making stunts stay in the air.

A lot of people were working on skills on the large mat, but I found a section that was free just as Connor, Matthew, and Gwen made their way to me. I knew working with them would make the assessment a breeze, considering hours of practice time we had logged together in the gym. We had all been in a skills class together through the winter, so even harder flying skills were becoming second nature for the groups of us. All of that was good for me, considering how I performed would determine if I landed on a level 5 team or not. And a spot on a level 5 team would allow me to finally compete at Worlds, the most coveted international cheerleading competition of the season.

"I want you to do a prep to extension lib, then a basic cradle out," Lenny instructed us with a smirk on his face. He knew we would be able to do the moves in our sleep if we wanted, but it was how assessments worked for flying. We had to start with the basics and move up as we were able. Thankfully it wasn't too long before we were getting to the harder stuff, including level 5 flying that I had only recently mastered.

"I want just Gwen and Matthew to base for this one," Lenny began explaining after trying a few intermediate skills. "I want to see a double around heel stretch, then drop down to prep level out of the skill. Next go back up for a double around to a scorpion. Hold it for three counts then move into a scale. Then I want to see a tick tock lib to a fortune cookie to ground. Connor I want you to step in after that for a basket to end it. Do you want to do a kick single, or go for the double?"

"Double," I said simply, and couldn't help but smile.

As I stood with Gwen and Matthew on either side of me, and Connor spotting us from behind, I realized how strange it was to be standing on the mat about to get lifted into the air. Even a few months ago, I would have needed Lenny to explain everything he had just told me over again and again. But now it was all second nature. I had a clear mental image of every pose and skill he listed, and knew holding them while high up in the air would be something I could accomplish without too much stress. In fact, all of it was so easy that I was back on the ground after completing the whole series of flying skills before I even had the chance to break a sweat.

"You're ridiculous Max," Lenny said with a dramatic eye roll once I was finished. "I don't know why they're even making you try out."

"I think she's just here so the rest of us get used to the idea of having her on one of our squads," Gwen suggested as she pulled her long brown hair into a tighter pony hair complete with a sparkly black cheer bow. "Fingers crossed she makes Bomb Squad."

"No way," Matthew replied. "She's totally going to make Nitro."

"Can we do partner stunts?" I asked Lenny, ignoring my friends play fighting about my team placements.

"Nope, not today," he said with a frown. "They want everyone to do the same series of skills so they can compare. But don't worry. You're going to be doing the one on one skills on a team soon enough."

I nodded, knowing he was likely right. All anyone had been talking about since Summit ended was what team they were going to be on for the following season. After seeing me compete on a junior level 3 and a senior level 4 team on the international stage in Florida, there wasn't a person in the gym that thought I wouldn't be placed onto a level 5 squad. The idea scared me at first, but the longer I started training in the weeks that led up to assessments, the more excited I was for the harder flying and tumbling skills that went with a level 5 team. No one was sure exactly which of the gyms' three level 5 teams I would be placed on, hence the fighting between my two friends.

"That was a great pass you did earlier," Connor assured me. He was walking with me off the mat as Matthew and Gwen continued to go back and forth.

"I didn't land the kick double," I reminded him quickly.

"That doesn't matter," he replied. "No one else all day has even had the guts to try it, let alone almost land it. Well, no one but you."

"Thanks, I think I really needed to hear that."

Connor took the opportunity to stop walking and give me a hug since we had already left the blue cheerleading mat. I was getting more and more used to hugs from my friends at the cheer gym, but sometimes it was strange. This was one of those times. Mostly because it felt like every time I was around Connor he had gotten taller than the last time I saw him. When I joined the gym, he was at least 5'5", a good 8 inches taller than me even then. But, in the few weeks leading up to the end of the season, and in the month since it had finished for good, he had grown at least another 3 or 4 inches. He was starting to push 6 feet, making me feel even more short and tiny next to him. Since, after all, his height also came with more muscles. Thankfully he still looked the same, with his curly dark brown hair, dark green eyes and dimples you could spot from a mile away.

"When are you going to stop getting taller?" I asked Connor as our hug finally ended. "I mean, I know I'm short and all, but now I feel like one of the seven dwarfs next to you."

"You're not that short," he challenged me with a smile. "Besides, you being tiny helped you get thrown extra high for that kick double."

I nodded, knowing he was right. In other sports I played over the years, I was made fun of or seen as a less capable athlete due to always being the shortest and thinnest girls on my teams, even when I wasn't the youngest. But at cheer, everything was different. Being small was a good thing, since you were easier to throw in the air or hold up high off the mat. So, as the smallest 13-year-old at the gym, my size was another thing that would likely help me get placed onto a level 5 squad finally.

"Did you do your jumps yet?" Connor asked as we turned and looked around at the other athletes still performing assessments. The group was slowly thinning out as people finished their skills and headed home.

"Yeah," I said with a nod of my head. "I wanted to get them out of the way first since they're my weakest area."

"You did great, I'm sure," he said before giving me a quick side hug. Then, knowing he needed to get back to basing, he turned and walk back onto the tumbling mat.

Despite being done with my assessments I didn't feel quite ready to head home. That could have been largely because I was used to hours of practice for Blast or Fuze multiple days of the week all last season. Or because of the hours and hours I logged at open gyms since returning home from Summit. Either way, I was free to go, but found myself torn. With all the other athletes still working, it felt strange to just leave.

"Hey Max," Lenny called out to me, as if sensing my hesitation. "Can you come fly for a bit? I have some more athletes that need to try their hand at basing, and you're light enough that even the shorter girls should be able to lift you."

"Okay," I grinned, excited for a reason to stay at the gym longer. Something I never could have imagined thinking even a year ago when I first joined the TNT Force gym.